Edie's Books

PARANORMAL

Dragon Blues
Dragon Mama Blues
Cattitude
The Fat Cat, a Cattitude short story
Dead People
Dead People in Love, a Dead People short story

SCIENCE FICTION ROMANCE

Galaxy Girls
Mixing It Up, a Galaxy Girls novella
The Kiss, a Galaxy Girls short story

Rules of Love & Murder

LOVE & MURDER, BOOK 2

Edie Ramer

Published by Blue Walrus Books

ISBN-13: 978-1-939328-25-0

Cover design by EJR Digital Art
Copy-editing by Blue Otter Editing
Proofreading by Judicious Designs
Formatting by Author E.M.S.

Published in the United States of America

One

August Reyes was eight years old and scared. Not as scared as last night, but still worried and fearful, like there was a ball covered with needles stuck inside his chest. Outside the car window, he saw trees and snow. There was hardly any traffic, and he was used to the sounds of traffic— along with the sounds of loud drunks and angry swearing and police sirens.

And sometimes...like last night...gunshots.

He was cold, too, in the backseat of the car. Really, really cold. The heater in the old Ford only blew warm air up at the front window and not downward, and it didn't reach the backseat, where he sat with his feet feeling like lumps of ice.

At first, he'd been happy when his mother had packed up and said they were leaving Chicago. Happy that they were going to a place where gunfire wouldn't wake him up in the middle of the night, his heart pounding in his chest like sticks hitting a donkey piñata.

A place where a bullet wouldn't kill his best friend in the apartment next door.

1

Where he didn't hear the police and the ambulance sirens.

His mom promised it wouldn't happen again. Told him she would take him someplace safe, even as the wails of Ricky's mom and his sisters' cries penetrated their thin walls, making him sick inside.

August had cried, too, even though he was too old to cry.

His mom had cried with him, tears running down her face that everyone said was beautiful. "Some things you're supposed to cry about," she said. "No matter how old you are. No matter if you're a boy or a man."

So now they were far away from the city. And he didn't know why she was taking them to this place that was all ice and snow. The trees had no leaves. Even though he could see it was beautiful, it was a cold beauty.

He didn't like cold. He didn't want cold. He wanted warmth and sun and green trees.

A place that looked like an island would be nice.

This place looked like a frozen planet in a movie where everyone was dying. This place wasn't nice.

"Mom, why can't we go someplace warmer?"

She laughed, but the sound was shaky like the car. She liked to say that her driving scared the car, and that's why it shook like a hula dancer.

"I heard about this place at the motel," she said. "I was cleaning a room, and the lady was on the phone, saying she was just back from paradise. When she left, there was a brochure on the desk in the room, and it said Door County."

He thought that even the name of the place—Door County—sounded like an open freezer door, but he nodded.

At least no one was shooting at him here.

"There were lots of stores and restaurants and places to stay in the brochure," his mom continued, but her voice was strangled. Worried. They were in Door County already—she had pointed out the sign to him as they'd passed it—and they had driven through two towns so far. But it didn't look like a place August would want to live. A lot of stores were closed, and there were only a few cars on the road.

Now, they must be between towns because there was just the road, with no houses and the trees on the sides of the road had no leaves. In some places, to his left, he could see icy waters. His mom said that the brochure she'd picked up at the hotel had a map of Door County on one page, and it had looked like a long finger. On one side was Lake Michigan, she said, and on the side they were driving on, there was a run-off from Lake Michigan that ran all the way into the city of Green Bay. And even though the city of Green Bay wasn't in Door County, they were on the Green Bay side of Door County now.

It didn't make sense to him. If the Green Bay waters were here, then they should be in Green Bay. But his mom didn't lie, though maybe the brochure did. Maybe they were in some magical place, and wizards and witches would fly down from the top of a tree and kill them.

Or maybe they would save them.

"Maybe in the next town there will be more

people," his mom said. "Maybe we can find a place to stay tonight."

He looked out the window again. Back in the real world, because he heard the worry in his mom's voice. She was probably worried about paying some of their precious money for a motel. And he kept thinking of Ricky. Yesterday, he'd walked home from school with Ricky. He'd stopped at Ricky's apartment and watched TV with Ricky while he waited for his mom to come home. Ricky's three sisters were older and they'd come home later, too.

So much had changed since then. He would never see Ricky again.

His chest ached. His mom always said God was good—but how could a good God allow this?

The car had been shaking off and on since they'd left Chicago and then Milwaukee. That seemed a long time ago. It started to shake again now, only this time it was worse.

He looked at his mom, and the lower part of her face was stiff, her teeth clenched as if she could hold the old car together just by prayer and her fierce will.

The car shook harder.

He bit down on his teeth and curled his hands tightly on his lap. He could be fierce, too.

And he could pray, too. *God, help us. Please help us. If you can help, I promise I'll be good forever.*

The car shook harder and faster. His mom, who never whimpered, made a scared sound.

He closed his eyes tighter. *Please, God, please. Whatever is wrong with the car, please fix it.*

But instead, the car shook like he imagined an earthquake would feel, with the ground breaking apart. His mother made an anguished sound, and she steered the car to the side of the road. As they reached it, there was one more quake and then...

Nothing.

His mom didn't say anything for a moment. Neither did he as he stared at her, holding his breath in, afraid to breathe.

She turned to him and gave him a smile that wasn't a real smile. He always thought his mother was beautiful, but right now her skin that normally was a pretty golden color looked yellow, her eyes too large and too scared.

His breath whooshed out. "Mama?" he asked. "Mama?"

"We're going to be okay. Someone will come by and help us. You'll see."

Two

"Mom! There's a lady waving at us."

The sunlight was dimming, the sky the color of smoke. But peering out of the back window, Elle could clearly see a dark-haired lady on the edge of the road ahead of them waving. Instead of slowing, her mom steered toward the middle of the road.

Elle and her mom knew most of the people in the area, at least in winter. In summer, when the tourists came, it was different. Not this woman. At age six, Elle was smart enough to know she'd never seen her before.

As they passed the woman, her mom drove slowly. Elle's face was so close to the window that she felt cold air, and she could see the sadness on the woman's face. More than that, she saw fear and desperation.

That was the same way Elle had felt inside her tummy at her daddy's funeral.

As the car cruised past the woman, her large eyes connected with Elle's. Pleading.

And then Elle saw *him*, at his mom's side. The boy. Looking straight at her, too. Even in the dim light, she could tell he was holding back a cry. Like she'd done at her dad's funeral when everyone said what a brave girl she was. And she wanted to yell at them that she wasn't brave. She wanted to lie on the ground of the cemetery and kick her feet and punch her fists and scream and scream and scream.

But she didn't do it. She'd promised her mom she would be brave.

No one could help her get her dad back. But maybe this one time, she could help the boy.

Her dad had joined the Marines to save people from bad things. She couldn't go and fight a war, not when she was so little, but she could try to help the lady and the boy.

She turned to her mom, bending forward as far as she could in her child's seat that she hated because she wanted to be a big girl. "There's a boy with her. Mom, he looks cold."

Her mother continued to drive, not slowing.

"Mom, the weather lady said it was freezing out."

"Honey, I can't stop."

"Yes, you can, Mom. You have to."

"Honey—"

Fear built up inside Elle, a terrible, terrible fear. "What if the boy freezes to death?" Her voice rose. "What if no one else comes by to save them?" She could see the side of her mom's face and the tightness of her mouth, the way it looked just before she blurted out, "No."

Then her mom's chin quivered. Just a tiny bit, but Elle's heart thumped harder.

"What if they die?" Elle said even louder. "Like Daddy? What if they die like him?"

"Honey..." Her mom slowed, and she steered the car to the side, and she made a laugh that was a cry and a laugh together. "Okay, we'll go back. You look behind us, and if you see anyone besides the boy and the woman, I want you to tell me. Okay?"

"Okay," Elle said, even though when she looked behind her, she could only see the top of the booster seat. But she knew how to undo the seat belt—her first grade teacher called her "precocious," which Elle thought must mean *smart*. So she unclipped the belt and pushed off the seat, then climbed onto the backseat and looked out of the window.

"Elle!" her mom said.

"I have to see. You said I have to see."

And she did see. The boy and the woman holding hands and looking at them. The woman looked afraid. The boy just looked like Elle thought a soldier would look. Standing straight and still. As if he didn't know what would happen, but whatever it was, he would be brave like her dad had been brave.

The car stopped, and the window on the passenger side rolled down. As it did, Elle scrabbled down the backseat to the door on her mom's side of the car as her mom said, "Can I help—"

Elle opened the door.

"Elle!"

"Mom, they're cold. Can't you see that?" She jumped out onto the road and ran around the car, the cold an icy slap on her cheeks. "Come inside!" she called as she headed toward the woman and the boy. "Come inside. It's cold out here, but it's warm in our car."

Her mom groaned.

The woman shook her head, and tears spurted in her eyes. But Elle's gaze had already gone to the boy. He still had that brave look on his face, but now his lips pressed together and quivered.

The woman looked to the open window, at Elle's mom, then back at Elle. She spoke in a thick voice, like grandma's butterscotch pudding. "Your mama is worried. I won't go into the car."

"But you're cold!" She stared at the boy. "Tell her."

"I'm not cold." The boy's teeth chattered, then the chattering stopped, and she knew he was biting down on his teeth.

Elle turned her face up to her mother's car. "Mom?"

Her mom mixed a laugh with a sigh. "Get in the car. All of you, please."

The boy went in the back with Elle and the woman in the front passenger seat. They stayed on the side of the road, the car not going anywhere. The boy's teeth started to chatter though Elle could hear the heater blasting. She noticed his mittens were made of yarn, not insulated like hers were.

He saw her staring. Scowling, he stuck his mittened hands inside his sleeves, his shoulders hunching up.

Was he mad at her?

She couldn't tell, but boys were odd. Her mom said boys were odd, too, so that must be true.

Except for her daddy. Her daddy had never

been odd, but she wished he'd never gone away to another country to save people there. She wished he had stayed home and played with her and kissed and hugged her.

She wished there were no more wars ever. No more killings. And no one's dad or mom got killed in wars ever again.

The tears were coming, and she turned forward, her face scrunched to hold them back. The boy's mom had been talking while she had looked at the boy, but her voice was low and soft, and she talked different from them. The words seemed to be the same as theirs, but it sounded like she was talking with her mouth full.

If Elle hadn't been looking at the boy so hard, her attention on him, maybe she would've made out what his mom was saying. Elle leaned forward and paid attention now, just in time to hear her mom sigh.

"I'm afraid you picked the wrong time of year to come here," her mom said. "In summer, yeah, the restaurants and hotels need help. Not now. Not this time of year. I don't—"

A sob came from the boy's mom. She put her hand over her face, and her head was shaking.

"Are you all right?" Elle's mom asked.

The woman didn't speak right away. Elle was aware of the boy next to her, and she was pretty sure he was holding his breath. Waiting to hear what his mom said next.

Slowly, her hand came down from her mouth. Slowly, she said with a heavy voice, "I have a little money, but I don't know if I can pay for the car.

There has to be something I can do. I can clean. I can—"

"What you can do," Elle's mom said, her words crisp, the way she talked when she made a decision, "is get your stuff from the car and put it in mine."

"We will pay you."

"I don't need your money. Elle and I will be leaving Trouble Bay soon, but I have an idea about a place where you can stay. Maybe a job, though I don't know if it will work out."

"Thank you. You are very kind." There were tears in the boy's mother's voice. She turned to the back of the car. "August—"

He was opening the door already. "I'll get our stuff." He jumped out, onto the road.

Elle didn't wait to hear what else the moms were going to say. She was sliding out of the car after him. "I'll help you. Wait for me! I'll help."

And inside her car, there was a sound that was either a sob or a laugh. She didn't know which mom it came from, but she wasn't going to look back to see who it was.

Instead, she was chasing after the boy.

Three

He would know her wrath.

Sylvia Pascal sat at the large conference room table with four other members of the unofficial and secret consortium who had named themselves The Founders of Trouble Bay. Not accurate, since they were actually a handful of the *descendants* of the original founders.

She and Angela Dufort, whose face resembled a bulldog's, were the only two women out of the five. Though even now, Sylvia wasn't certain that Miles Anderson should belong to the group, as his great-grandfather had only been part of the Wisconsin town since 1906. The others had insisted that Miles be included. He owned gas stations and grocery stores in Trouble Bay and two other Door County communities. The others had said that no matter what the economy, people had to eat and gas up.

Sylvia pinched her lips together. As long as they kept the big box stores out of Trouble Bay, Miles wouldn't have to scrub toilets in his ancestral home, as she was doing. All this because of Charley—her lying, cheating, often drunken, and no-longer-alive husband.

She took a deep breath, wiping out the image of Charley as he lay in the parking lot of the tavern, fall leaves on his body, the hole in his left chest bleeding out in a surprisingly thin stream.

Even though his murder—and his activities before his murder—had put her in the middle of gossip, she'd felt a bit sorry for him. She wasn't inhuman. He'd been weak and stupid, but he was the father of her son. Her chest had even pinched a little.

When the deputies had come to her house the next morning, she had allowed tears to flow as the police and nosy neighbors—and even a few stray tourists—watched her from the sidewalk. She didn't like to show her weaknesses, but tears would make others sympathetic. Especially if she didn't blubber. Silent tears were more effective than noisy tears.

And if she hadn't cried, some people might have wondered if she had found out about his extramarital activities and had killed him. Even without proof, the insurance company might have balked at paying her.

The next week she'd found out that, ten months previously, he'd cashed in his life insurance policy.

That had stopped any urge to cry. If there were a money repellent, Charley had oozed it out of his pores.

Some men deserved to die young.

The sheriff still hadn't found Charley's killer. Certainly there was a list of people who would have liked him to stop breathing. She wasn't the only one who might have felt the urge to stop the beating of Charley's heart with a bullet.

She'd married a golden prince, only to find out that life wasn't a fairy tale, and what she had thought was gold was fool's gold—which had made her a fool.

And now another man had disappointed her.

"What did Duke say?" John Norman asked. A property developer, he came from a long line of Normans who couldn't seem to do wrong. At least, not when it came to business. John was a husky man in his mid-thirties with permanent frown lines on his forehead. His wife, Janet, was vocal in her complaints about his sexual prowess. Every Sunday and Wednesday evening, an hour after dinner and over in four minutes.

Sylvia liked knowing his inadequacies. When he expounded on the things they needed to do— which was too often—she would sometimes go over his wife's comments in her mind and smile calmly.

Her husband may have been a liar and a cheater, but at least he'd been good in bed.

John and the other two men liked to think they ran the consortium to keep the newcomers out of the government planning and the town founders in, but Sylvia was the one who'd brought them together. John, of course, was the town board chairman. Sylvia had known it would happen. Money did buy power, and John Norman loved power. She was the planning commission chairperson, which she thought had more practical power.

"Sylvia?" John asked. "Did you hear me?"

"Yes, I heard you," she said. "And, no, Duke emphatically said he isn't interested in joining us."

"I told you that it's too early after his wife's death," Angela said.

Sylvia gripped the pencil. Was that a dig at her for starting the consortium with the others so soon after Charley's demise?

"It's been six months since the accident," Sylvia said and felt a little pang. She'd *liked* Leah. They were sisters-in-law and knew each other well. Though Sylvia was confident that she would be a more suitable match for Duke than her dumpy relative through marriage, she had been genuinely sorry when she'd heard about Leah's death.

"I'm still grieving over the loss of Fred." Angela managed a sniff that sounded suspiciously false to Sylvia. "And that was more than a year ago."

"'Course you are." Brad Patton, who owned a landscaping design company, clumsily patted her shoulder. "I still miss my Molly, too."

"Ooh." Angela gave him a melting look.

Sylvia shivered. How odd that so many of their spouses were dead.

They couldn't all have... No, of course not. That would be...well, a bit odd.

"Angela is right," John said. "Try talking to Duke again in six months."

She nodded. Of course she would try again. It was going to take longer than she'd thought to pull him into line, but when she decided to do something, nothing stopped her. Duke had married Leah, a short and curvy woman, the summer after they'd graduated from college. It hadn't taken many years for Leah to turn dumpy. Not like Charley, who'd remained tall and fit until he died. Leah had taken after her mother, and Charley had taken after their father.

As the years had passed, most townspeople had suspected that Leah wasn't able to have babies. But Sylvia's mother-in-law had told Sylvia in confidence that Duke had a low sperm count, and he was the reason behind Duke and Leah's childlessness.

When Sylvia had stopped off to Duke's hotel, she'd thought he would be glad to see her. After all, she was an old friend as well as related by marriage. And her eight-year-old son, Charles Jr.—who insisted they call him Chuck—might have a shot at inheriting Duke's resort, the biggest and most prosperous in Trouble Bay, with its own restaurant and docks.

But Sylvia didn't take anything for granted. Duke was only thirty-nine. In his prime, but at the age where a man thought about his legacy.

So why not hook up with a relative-through-marriage who had always carried herself with dignity?

A woman who lived by a set of rules?

A woman whose spouse had also died tragically?

A woman whose son had the same blood running through him as his beloved late wife?

"You're much more attractive than Leah," John said, his voice and the look he gave her cool and assessing.

She inclined her head, not thanking him. There was no flirtation in his voice or admiration in his eyes. He was stating a fact, and she took it as such. She had no false modesty and knew she was attractive in a youngish Grace Kelly way. She liked to conduct herself like a queen, too, with grace and restraint.

And, when necessary, retribution.

"Perhaps I should be the one to talk to him," Angela said, her tone defensive. "I was friends with Leah. And I believe we might be related through marriage."

Sylvia managed not to roll her eyes. Really? Angela was hoping that Duke would turn to her? Though Duke liked dogs, Sylvia doubted he would want to marry a woman who resembled one.

"Leave it to Sylvia," John said, his tone gruff. "Gary and I have already approached Duke, and he wasn't receptive to us. We don't want him to think we're ganging up on him."

Angela set her lips together, lines bracketing them, clearly not happy. But unless she was eating chocolate—or cake or cookies—Angela was not likely to exude happiness.

John turned to Sylvia and looked her up and down. The frown on his forehead deepened. "Three months might be better. This time, perhaps wear something that's...more...um..."

"Sexier," Gary said. "Wear something sexy."

The men chuckled, and Angela's lips tightened.

Beyond a slight lifting of her chin, Sylvia showed no emotion. Men were foolish. She'd already known this. It was just too bad more of them weren't found lying on the cold ground with a bullet in their chests. Because, as she could attest, men drove women to murder.

Four

They'd stayed overnight at the small house in Trouble Bay. August slept in a sleeping bag in a room with a sewing machine and a desk with a computer on it. His mom slept on the couch. He was glad the house wasn't too big or too fancy, like homes on TV. It made Mrs. Styles and Elle seem more like him and his mom. As if they weren't too much better than them.

He wanted to tell his mom, but she would think that he was insulting Mrs. Styles, who was being so kind to them—stopping her car when they were standing on the side of the road, like two frozen Popsicles. And he didn't want to insult Mrs. Styles. It was just that... Well, he didn't know what it meant, but he knew enough to not say anything.

His mom already thought that Elle's mom was an angel for taking them into her home and then feeding them and letting them stay overnight. Maybe she was. Mrs. Styles and her daughter, Elle.

Elle had told him last night that her dad had died in Afghanistan. August didn't really wish that his own dad was dead. His dad had left them when August was three "to go back to Mexico where it was sunny and warm," he said in the note that he'd left for August's mom.

But if someone's father had to be dead, why shouldn't it have been his instead of Elle's?

His mom said God did everything for a reason, but August couldn't see any good reason for that.

After a breakfast of eggs and toast, Mrs. Styles said she was going to see if someone could help August and his mom. Then she hesitated, standing in the kitchen with the black-and-white-tiled floor, her forehead furrowed as she looked from his mom to Elle, who sat next to him at the table.

It felt odd to August to be in this kitchen, especially on a Sunday. Usually on Sundays, his mom didn't have to work a second job at the hotel, and he didn't have to wait in the lobby for her, with the desk clerk acting as his babysitter because his mom didn't want to leave him alone. On the days she wasn't scheduled to work on a Sunday, they would be at church.

Maybe Mrs. Styles was the same and this was why she didn't leave right away.

"I'll take good care of her. I promise." His mom held her head high as she looked straight into Mrs. Styles's eyes.

Mrs. Styles hesitated another moment, then nodded and left.

Only then did he realize she worried that they might be bad people. That they might steal things and hurt Elle.

He grew flushed but not angry. She was being careful. He understood that. Mrs. Styles didn't know him or his mom, yet she'd let them into her house.

Ricky's mom used to say, "Never trust anyone you don't know well."

Someone they didn't know had killed Ricky. The police had said it was random.

Random was a terrible word. It meant the shooter hadn't known Ricky. Hadn't cared about him. The police even said it might have been an accident.

Accident? Killing a boy by accident? Like it was just a mistake and shouldn't matter?

It mattered. It mattered a lot. Just thinking about it, August's head heated, and he looked away, at the white stove with the black spiral electric burners.

Ricky could've grown up to be...anything he wanted to be. But a stray bullet had stopped him from growing up. Stopped his lungs from breathing. Stopped his heart from beating.

A small hand touched his arm. "What are you thinking?"

He looked sideways. "Nothing."

Elle's nose scrunched. "When my dad used to tell my mom 'nothing,' she would say, 'that means you have an empty head.'"

August's mom laughed, and August relaxed, the tightness in his belly loosening. It was the first time he'd heard his mom laugh since the shooting.

"Do you have a game?" he asked Elle. If she played a game with him, she wouldn't be asking him what he was thinking. Though Elle talked like an older girl, she was little. Not even coming up to his chin. Her hair, the color of a ripe orange, sprang out in curls all over, and she had freckles on her face, and she hopped from one foot to the other. She made him think of a puppy that couldn't stand still.

But she wasn't a puppy. She was a girl. A person.

One who'd saved his life and his mom's. A person like no one he'd seen before.

Her mouth curved down now. "They're packed away."

"Packed? Are you going away?"

She nodded vigorously. It seemed to him that she did everything vigorously, as if she had extra energy packed inside her. While he thought before he acted, he already knew she acted before she thought.

"My mom has a new job, working at the university Madison. We rented an apartment, and my mom will take classes, and she said when I'm older, I can take classes, too."

"Classes to do what?"

"To write! I want to be a writer."

"A famous writer?" he asked.

"Maybe. Or an ice skater. I like ice skating, too."

"You don't fall?"

"*Everyone* falls. That's what my mom tells me. When I fall, I just get back up again."

He nodded, as if he knew, though he'd never ice skated. "What kind of stories do you write?"

"I wrote a story already." She jumped up a little, like she had springs on the bottom of her tennis shoes. "Want to hear it?"

He nodded. It would fill in the time before her mother came back. Anything would be better than waiting to see what would happen next.

She beamed at him, and it made him think of the sun shining brightly. Then she turned and ran up the stairs, her feet in her slippers making a lot of noise for a skinny little girl. At the top of the stairs, a gray cat that she called Silver meowed.

"She's a good girl," August's mom said. "And you're a good boy, too."

He ducked his head. He didn't feel good inside. Inside, he felt sick. Inside, he wished he had a gun, and he could shoot the assholes who had killed Ricky. *Asshole* was a word that he wasn't supposed to use, but he knew all those forbidden words. Anyone who lived in his neighborhood had heard them used often by the time they were able to talk.

But if he said them, his mom would be angry. So he kept his mouth shut, but in his mind, he shouted them.

Asshole.

Fucker.

Shithead.

And the word his mother said was the worst of all, like bullets shooting off in his mind: *Hate, hate, hate, hate, hate—*

"Here it is." Footsteps clambered down the stairway.

The thought that she wasn't scared of making noise had him smiling as Elle and her cat rushed into the front room. Elle glowed, her blue eyes shining, her smile brilliant, her orange hair like the first rays of sunlight in the morning.

She looked unreal. Not like anyone he knew, but like a girl in a fairy tale. A girl from a fairyland.

No, that was too girly, and she wasn't girly like a fairy. An elf-girl fit her better.

All of his muscles relaxed. He could even feel his heart relax, too. He breathed easier now. Like he didn't have to worry all the time that bad things would happen.

Maybe Elle was his good luck elf-girl.

She rushed over to the gray-green couch his mom had slept on, and she bounced onto the middle cushion. She patted the cushion next to her. "Come over. I'll read to you." She turned to his mom, who was standing by the front window. "You, too, Mrs. Reyes. I can read to you, too. It's a story about a fish and a cat and a dog. Would you like to hear it?"

"I would love to," his mom said in her accent that he knew was thick, but neither Mrs. Styles nor Elle had seemed to notice. Their mouths didn't smirk and their noses didn't pinch in, as if they smelled something bad, like some ladies had done at the motel, making August flatten his lips together to keep from yelling at them.

He and his mom sat on either side of Elle, and she opened the notebook and read a story about a cat who found a fish on the sand, and the cat bent its nose down to the fish, who got scared and flopped around. Then a dog came running down the beach, kicking up sand—

"Because that's what dogs do," she said, lifting her head to him and then his mom.

They both nodded, and she proceeded to go on

with her story as the fish and the cat and the dog all talked to each other.

He was sure that in real life the cat would eat the fish, even though the cat promised she wouldn't. In real life, if the dog was really hungry, maybe the dog would eat it, too. He'd seen dogs eat garbage in an alley. They ate anything.

And while they had scarfed down the garbage, his stomach had made a noise. A hungry noise.

But his stomach was full now, and he didn't say anything. This was Elle's story. He knew enough about girls to know that when they were telling their story, they didn't want a boy taking it over and telling it his way.

She started talking again, and he bent his head toward her, silently admitting that he wanted to know the fish's fate.

The fish was flopping a little less now.

That wasn't good. He knew that. It wasn't good at all.

Then the dog started to talk, and now August was sure that the dog would eat the fish.

Before Elle could say what it was, the roar of a bad car engine on the road in the front of the house stopped her in mid-word. He twisted toward the window but he was too short to see unless he stood. Instead, he listened and heard a car door open and then slam shut, the sound carrying to them in the frigid air.

His insides tightened. He felt Elle's gaze on him, but he shifted on the couch and stared at the front door.

It must be Elle's mom already. That had been fast.

Was that good? Or bad?

He didn't know, and he hated that he didn't know. He was just a kid, and he couldn't fix everything. He curled his fists at his sides, because he wanted to fix everything. He wanted to fix it for his mom. He wanted to fix it for himself.

His mom stood, and he pushed off the couch and stood next to her. Though he was too big to hold her hand—he was eight, after all—she reached for his hand and clasped her fingers around his, and he squeezed his around hers.

It was just the two of them. It had been the two of them for a long time. He could hardly remember his dad. A tall man who'd made his mom cry. For a long time, August had hated him. But now he was just scared.

Their future depended on whatever Mrs. Styles would say.

Please. Please. Please.

From the couch came a scuffling noise, then the sound of Elle hopping onto the floor. He didn't glance around. He just held his mother's hand and stared at the door.

Still, he was aware of Elle stepping up to his side, and then, as the door handle turned and he stopped breathing, Elle's small hand took his, her fingers only long enough to clutch three of his. He could have pulled away easily, but he closed his fingers around hers, too.

As the door opened and Elle's mom stepped inside, he was holding both his mom's and Elle's hands.

Mrs. Styles shut the door behind her, not

saying anything, her face looking serious. Too serious. And then...she smiled.

Elle jumped up and down and gave a scream. A happy scream.

He let go of her hand. His mom was still gripping his, and emotion filled his chest. He didn't know what had happened, but it had to be good news or Mrs. Styles wouldn't smile at them. They wouldn't be stuck with no car and no money and no place to go in this cold and snowy place. Her smile told him that they had somewhere to go.

His breath whooshed out, and so did his mom's. She stepped toward Mrs. Styles, holding out her arms.

"Thank you for helping us. Thank you. Thank you."

"It's you I should be thanking." Mrs. Styles's cheeks turned pink. "I let Duke believe he needed to help you, but, really, I've been worried about him."

"Me, too," Elle said.

August turned toward her, and she looked up at him, the smile gone from her face and her eyes.

Odd, she looked almost plain without the smile, when just seconds ago, she'd looked pretty.

"Uncle Duke is sad," she said. "Very sad."

"His wife died." Mrs. Styles's voice lowered, the way people did when they talked about something bad. "Leah was a good friend of mine. It's been six months since she died, and he's still not over it."

"He owns a big place." Elle opened up her arms wide on each side. "It's a resort. Resorts are really big. Bigger than a lodge."

He didn't say anything, but he thought that was going to be a lot of rooms to clean. He squared his shoulders.

If it were too many for his mom to clean, he would—

"Don't worry about taking care of the rooms," Mrs. Styles said. "They're all closed. Duke hasn't had any guests since the end of summer. He closed up the house he'd shared with Leah, and now he's all alone in one of the rooms of the resort. Hardly eating, by the look of him. Skinnier every time I see him."

Elle nodded vigorously. "Uncle Duke is very sad. He cried at the funeral. I cried, too, and so did Mom."

Mrs. Styles laughed but there was a thick sorrow in the laughter. "Yes, we did cry, honey. We loved Leah."

August's mom took another step toward Mrs. Styles, who still had her coat buttoned, her black scarf dangling from her hands.

"Don't worry," August's mom said. "I will take good care of him. Me and August. That's a promise."

August nodded. He didn't promise out loud, but in his heart, he promised.

And he always kept his promises.

But first...

He turned to Elle. "What happened to the fish?"

She beamed. "You'll have to read the rest of the story."

Five

"You'll like living with Uncle Duke." Elle made her voice quiet in the backseat of mother's car on the way to her uncle's resort. It was Sunday, but her mom said that they would miss church today. They had other things to do, and she said God would approve.

Elle peered out of the window, not wanting to think about the sad times. The sky was a cold blue, and there was snow on the ground. The bright sun shone down on them, but it was a cold sun. Way too far away to warm them. In the backseat with her, August didn't say anything, but Elle could tell he was scared.

Maybe *scared* wasn't the right word. *Worried.* That was the right word, and she liked to get her words right. Words mattered.

"Uncle Duke has a dog," she continued. "Two dogs. If you ask him nicely, he'll let you walk them."

August turned to look at her. Because he wasn't in a booster seat like she was, their eyes were level. "He's your uncle?" he asked.

"Not a real uncle. He's my dad's cousin, so he's

almost an uncle. And he was married to my mom's best friend. Aunt Leah. She's dead, too. She had an accident and died. It was very sad."

Her mom turned into the resort's driveway that led to the parking lot. August looked ahead and his breath sucked in. She sat straighter and tried to see it through his eyes. The resort was a big, golden-bricked, three-floor building that stretched a long way to the right and a long way to the left. They were looking at the back of the resort, but she liked the front even more. The front had a view of the bay and the docked boats, and the suites on the second and third floors had patios so the guests could look out at the bay. Sometimes in winter, Elle and her mom would drive here on weekends and swim in the indoor pool. When they moved to Madison, Elle would miss her swims.

"Your cousin rents all these rooms?" August's mom asked, and her voice sounded awed.

"Duke doesn't rent rooms." Her mom's voice carried to the back. "He rents *suites.*"

"Mom, sweets are like candy and cookies, aren't they?" Elle giggled. "How can Uncle Duke rent candy?"

Her mother groaned. "You're always asking what things mean."

"How am I supposed to know if I don't ask?"

Elle could feel August's gaze on her, and her stomach clenched. Some of the other kids in her class thought she was weird.

She didn't want August to think she was weird, too.

Her mom was slowing down, heading toward the resort. "You want to know *everything*," her mom said.

Elle nodded. Yes, she did want to know everything. There was so much she needed to learn. And she didn't want to wait until later. She wanted to know *now*.

"Suites spelled s-u-i-t-e-s are like an apartment," her mom said. "They have small kitchens and a view of the bay. In summer, guests can go on the boats."

Elle turned back to August, who was peering out the window. When she'd read him her story this morning, he'd *listened* to her story. He'd told her that she should write stories, and she'd puffed up inside her chest and nodded, though she wasn't completely sure what she wanted to do when she was a grown-up. But she was happy that he *liked* her.

Sometimes the boys and the girls in her class looked at her as if there was something wrong in her head because she wasn't like them.

Some of them even made fun of her, but she ignored them. Most of the girls and boys liked her. And her mom said it was good to be different.

"Our car!" Mrs. Reyes cried out. "It's a miracle."

Elle leaned forward and saw the car parked by the entrance.

"Not a miracle," Elle's mom said. "Duke must've called the gas station and had them fix it."

"He's a saint." Mrs. Reyes's voice was thick again.

"Ha!" Elle's mom stopped the car. "No man's a

saint, but once in a while, they do something nice. Don't give Duke too much credit. All he had to do was pick up the phone. And it's good for him to think of someone besides himself. C'mon, let's go inside."

Six

August followed his mom and Mrs. Styles inside. Elle walked behind them, and his heart was thumping in his chest. This lobby was so different from the one in the motels where his mom had worked. Instead of being drab and rundown, this place was shiny and perfect. The wood on the counters and the window looked like it had been rubbed with lemon. The windows were tall and wide, the sunlight shining into the rooms, the floors like golden marble. Everything glowed.

He reminded himself that his mom was here to get a job. This wasn't a home. This wasn't even a full-time job—if she was offered one. This was temporary.

Footsteps came from the hall, and in the emptiness of the building, he could clearly hear shoes clomp. As a tall, lean man strode into the room, Elle's hand slid into his.

"I'm doing this for Robbie," the man with graying brown hair and sad eyes said. "He would've wanted me to do it."

"You don't have to sound like the Grinch," Mrs. Styles said in a disapproving voice that sounded just like his mom's when he'd said something wrong in church. Then Elle's mom turned and introduced August and his mom to Mr. Abbott, only she called him Duke.

August mumbled something and pulled his hand from Elle's. Babies and little kids held hands. He wasn't a baby.

"Robbie was my dad," Elle whispered. "Will you write me? Or email me?"

He nodded. She was a little weird, but he liked her. She was different. Different in a good way.

She beamed at him. "I'll write you back. Maybe I'll send you stories."

"Okay," he said, looking at his mom. No one had ever written him a letter before. He'd never written anyone a letter. He didn't know anyone who wrote letters.

"You can write me stories, too," she said.

He nodded slowly. He didn't want to write a story, but if not for her and her mom, he didn't know what would have happened to them.

On an impulse, he turned, put his arms around her arms, bent his head, and kissed her, his mouth closed.

He pulled back. Her eyes were big, and an odd sound was coming from her uncle. Like a rusty door opening.

They both turned to their moms and Elle's uncle, and August could see his eyes glistened and his mouth looked funny, as if he were going to cry. But instead, another sound came out that could've been a cry.

August took a step back.

"Duke?" Mrs. Styles said. "Are you *laughing*?"

The man's eyes crinkled. He didn't look at Elle's mom or his. Instead, he looked at August and Elle. "I can hardly believe it, but that's just what I was doing."

Elle took August's hand again and squeezed it. He was still scared, but she was a small girl, and if she could be brave, so could he.

"Uncle Duke?" she asked. "Are the dogs in the back? Can I show August your dogs?"

He sniffed, his laughter stopped, and gave August a hard stare. "You like dogs?"

August was tempted to look at his mother for a go-ahead nod, but the girl was already pulling him away. He braced his legs and nodded. "Yes," he said, making his voice firm. He liked Elle, but he didn't want a girl to speak for him. Especially a girl two years younger than him.

"All right." Her uncle nodded. "You two go ahead. The dogs are big, but they like kids."

"We like them, too." Elle pulled August away, and this time he let her. She was like his good luck charm.

And his good luck charm was going away soon, and he might never see her again.

Seven

Two years later

Sylvia stood in the Trouble Bay Gun Club indoor firing range with her eye protection on along with double ear protection—sponges and ear muffs. She liked her sharp hearing, and it was better to take an extra moment to do something right than to be lazy and do it wrong.

If only Charley had thought like her...

She banished that thought. This day wasn't about Charley. It was about the wedding this afternoon. Duke and Pilar. His cleaning lady.

Charley used to say that ice ran through her veins. She felt icy chills now as she lifted the gun, the only person here except for the kid watching her, making sure she wasn't going to shoot into the ceiling or do something stupid. As if.

Sylvia didn't do stupid. Even her marriage to Charley had looked like the smart thing to do at the time. And his resemblance to Prince Charming hadn't hurt.

Charley, Charley, Charley.

Over three years now that he'd been gone, but it was hard to forget him. Hard to forget what she'd done.

Not that she was sorry. The prince she'd married was, in reality, a womanizer and a bad businessman. A bad example for Chuck.

And as for Duke's wedding...

She held her Glock 19 in her right hand, aimed it at the target, leaned forward in a slight bend, her arm almost straight with another slight bend, and curled her left hand tightly over the bottom of the right to steady her aim and make sure the gun didn't jump.

Then she squeezed the trigger.

There wasn't much of a kick, but the power of shooting the gun vibrated through her.

She waited a few seconds to be steady, then squeezed the trigger again.

And again.

And again.

Counting as she shot.

Charley used to call her a bean counter, mocking her seriousness. She preferred to think of herself as a bullet counter.

Taking a little longer, she squeezed the trigger for the last bullet.

When she was done, the pulley retrieved the target, and she looked at it dispassionately. One bull's-eye and one in the ten-ring, the others grouped nearby.

No matter how she looked at it, the target was dead.

The other target drew up. One bullet had

nicked the bull's-eye. This time there were two in the ten-ring. Good. Very good.

She cleaned up the brass, then packed up and headed outside into the cold. She needed to fix her hair, get dressed, and put on her makeup. She also needed to practice smiling, because her son said that when she'd first heard the news at church, her smile had made him think of the Ice Queen.

He'd thought it was funny.

He hadn't realized how furious she was. He would never know that when she'd shot the target today, she was picturing Duke's face.

For the past two years, she'd been stopping off at Duke's home every few weeks, chatting for a few minutes, very subtly comparing their widowed circumstances and inviting him to come to her place for a home-cooked dinner anytime.

He'd never taken her up on it, but she'd thought she was making headway.

Fool.

What was wrong with her? After all these years, she was still a fool over a man.

But why would she have thought anything different? She knew her worth. She was nine years younger than Duke—practically another generation. She was blond and attractive and classy. She was what all men wanted. To top it off, she and Duke were related through marriage.

She was certainly a step up from his late wife, her sister-in-law, Leah. Leah had been addicted to romance books and chocolate. Her favorite clothes had been stretchy pants and a sweatshirt. Charley used to say Leah had the hips of a peasant, cheeks like a chipmunk, and a voice like a parrot who had sucked in the air from a helium balloon. And then there was her screechy, hurt-your-ears laugh, too.

Sylvia had liked Leah, but she'd never understood what Duke had seen in her.

And now, instead of turning to Sylvia, he was marrying an even more inappropriate woman.

Getting in the car, she seethed. Driving to her home, she seethed.

How dare he?

How *dare* he?

And more questions:

Why Pilar? His cleaning lady? Not that she had anything against any woman who did honest work. But why not her, the perfect woman?

She'd done everything right, but her life had gone so wrong.

Why was this happening to her again?

As she reached her home, the anger still simmered. She sat in her car parked in front of her beloved house that she shared with strangers. Instead of getting out of the car, she stared ahead at the rows of stores that catered to tourists. For the most part, they were closed for the winter, along with a few restaurants. A street for tourists, though this was her home, too, and her bed-and-breakfast was almost always booked solid from May to the middle of September. She was doing well. Especially now that Charley wasn't siphoning off her money.

Really, she didn't need a man.

She repeated that silently.

She didn't need a man.

In fact, she would've done much better so far if she hadn't married Charley. Of course, she had Chuck, and she wasn't sorry for that. She just couldn't stop feeling like a fool for chasing after Duke for the last two years, not once realizing he wasn't interested. That he'd *never* been interested.

She held her head high now and squared her shoulders.

It was *his* loss.

If he wanted to marry Pilar...well, that was his choice. His decision.

She wasn't going to ask herself *why* anymore.

Instead, tonight she was going to smile and dance and eat, because she'd had a revelation. She was a powerful woman, and powerful women didn't need a man.

So fuck them. Fuck every single one who'd mocked her for acting prissy when she was growing up. Fuck them all.

She would show them. She would be rich. She would be independent. She would be alone. And she would like it.

She made a decision. A vow to herself that she would never need a man again.

If she ever did decide that a man was good enough for her, he would have to be someone special. Because she was someone special, and she deserved a man as wonderful as herself.

Eight

"You look like a princess in a fairy tale," August said.

Elle laughed and jumped up and down. The wedding cake had been yummy, and she'd been the flower girl at the wedding in her pink dress, even though Mrs. Pascal said that eight was too old to be a flower girl. When she'd told her mom, her mom had narrowed her eyes at Mrs. Pascal, and Elle could tell she wanted to say bad words to her. Turning back to Elle, her mom had said in a hard voice, "No one with any sense cares how old the flower girl is. Or how young. Okay?"

She'd nodded. When her mom said *okay* like that, Elle always nodded, and then filed it away in her mind.

She was never too old to do what she wanted.

Or too young.

Age didn't matter.

"I'd rather be a princess warrior," she said to August now. Around them the waiters were moving the tables so they could dance. Elle jumped up again. She could hardly wait. She liked to dance, even if she didn't know the steps. She could make up her own.

"Move it, warrior princess," one of the tall and skinny Hampton boys said. The boys' mom was an artist, and they lived in a small cottage not too far from the house where Elle used to live. The reception was in the big room at Uncle Duke's resort, and he'd hired local teenage boys to help out. She'd been going to weddings here since she could remember, and she knew what was going to happen next.

She backed up and stuck her tongue out at the Hampton boy. He stuck his tongue out at her, then he and his brother laughed, and so did she.

Weddings were fun!

When she turned back to August, he was frowning.

"Aren't you glad your mom married Uncle Duke?" she asked.

"I am." But the creases in his forehead deepened.

"Then what's wrong?"

He shrugged, and she put her hands on her hips and narrowed her eyes.

"What's wrong?" she asked again. Boys didn't like to tell girls everything, so sometimes girls had to ask until the boys told them.

"Some people are saying that my mom is marrying Duke for money. It makes me angry."

"Who said that?" She looked around at all the grown-ups. The women were wearing pretty dresses, and the men were dressed nice, too. "Tell me who they are, and I'll kick them."

He snorted a laugh. "I'd like to see that."

She jumped up and down, but this time with stubbornness. "Tell me. I'll do it."

He laughed out loud now. "You can't do it."

"Yes, I can. I can do anything."

Laughter came from behind her. The Hampton boys again. They were laughing at her, but she didn't care, because she could do anything.

And they couldn't. They were boys, and girls were better than boys.

"I don't want you to kick anyone." August took a deep breath, his skinny chest beneath the light blue, button-down shirt puffing out.

The last time she saw him was during a short visit in the summer. Since then, he'd had a growth spurt, and he looked older than his ten years. Elle's mom kept saying she would have a growth spurt, but so far it hadn't happened.

She went into a karate pose. "I'm taking karate lessons. I can make them sorry."

"You are?" His eyes like dark chocolate brightened.

"Yes." She jumped up and down again—just because she felt excited and she liked jumping. "You want to take karate lessons, too? It's fun."

His smile went away, and he looked down. "I don't think I should ask Duke for lessons."

"Sure, you can." She grabbed his sleeve. "Come on. Let's ask."

"No." He stepped back, pulling his sleeve out of her hand. "I won't ask him."

She frowned.

"I'm going to go to the bathroom." He headed toward the door nearest them.

Elle watched him leave. When he turned into the hallway, she marched to the front of the room, where Uncle Duke and Aunt Pilar sat, holding hands and looking flushed and happy.

Everyone should be happy today. Even August.

She walked faster, but then she thought he might be back soon, and she ran to them.

Nine

When August returned to the reception room, he could see straight through the end of the room where his mom and new dad stood in front of a fieldstone fireplace, bending a little to talk to the girl with the red, coiling hair who stood in front of them.

The redhead talked, her arms flailing. He couldn't see her face, but he knew it was animated. His parents' faces were serious as they listened to her and then responded. They seemed to be in a very intense conversation.

He strode toward them, and no one else mattered. Just him and just them. All the noise around him was a blurred buzz, and he didn't even have to walk around anyone. It felt as if people saw him coming and got out of his way. Kind of like the sea parting for Moses.

His mom saw him first, straightening, her eyes lighting up. Happy to see him.

He didn't know what to feel. Not because of his mom, but because of the girl. Elle.

She was different from anyone he knew. So smiley and happy, even though she wasn't rich.

He knew that. And her dad, a Marine, had been killed overseas. He knew that, too.

He raised his head and squared his shoulders and strode faster.

By the time he reached them, they were all beaming at him.

"August," his mom said, "your dad and I have a surprise for you,"

Elle jumped up and down, as if she were a small kid instead of eight already. She put her hands over her mouth, but a squeal of happiness stole through her fingers.

August looked at his mom, waiting.

"We've had some wonderful gifts today," Duke said in his warm voice that was so different from the distant one that he'd used when they'd first come here. "But my most wonderful gift is you and your mother."

August's mom sniffed, and August wiped his knuckles under his nose. He vowed to himself that he was not going to get weepy. Not here. Too many people would see him cry like a baby.

"Your mother and I would like to give you a gift, too." He peered over his shoulder at August's mother. "Isn't that right, Pilar?"

She nodded, and her eyes shone with tears, but August knew from the way she beamed at him that they were happy tears.

Duke turned back to him. "We've heard from a little birdie that you want to take karate lessons."

August looked at Elle, and she beamed brighter.

His throat got tighter, and he looked back at Duke, who was smiling at him with kindness. He was a tall man, and his medium-sized mom looked up to him with melting eyes.

Duke's eyes melted at her, too.

It felt weird to see his mom so happy. It hadn't happened all at once, but slowly. Like ice melting over a long winter, and all of a sudden it was spring and you're walking in sunshine. And you don't know how it happened, but you're happy that spring and the green leaves and the warm sun are there.

That's how it was between his mom and Duke. A slow thaw of their frozen hearts.

He looked down, wondering where that thought came from. It was like something he'd read on a mushy card. Not something he would ever say to his mom.

"Your mom and I," Duke continued, "want to give you a gift. We already have something picked out to give you tomorrow, but you're such a great kid, we want to give you something else." He straightened and held out his hand to August's mother. "You tell him."

She took his hand. "I have a very smart son. I'm sure he's already guessed that he's getting karate lessons."

He nodded, then had to clear his throat to thank them.

"You'll kick my butt in no time." Duke winked, and August swallowed. All day he'd been vibrating with a secret anxiety. And now, just like that, he wasn't vibrating anymore.

It finally hit him that everything was going to be all right.

That all this good stuff wasn't going to disappear.

He'd liked Duke from the start, even though Duke hadn't spoken much then. Maybe because they were both hurting. Duke because of his first wife's death. August because of his friend. And Duke had let him play with his two dogs, Sasha, a golden retriever, and Nelson, a smaller and sturdier black-and-white dog who drooled and no one could tell what breed he was, except that he liked everybody and ate anything.

And now, Duke was going to be his dad.

An older man and woman came up to his mom and Duke. As the grown-ups talked, Elle skipped toward August.

He wondered what he was going to say to her.

"The next time I come," she said, "we can fight each other."

He laughed, and she laughed, too, her cheeks scrunching up.

"You want more cake?" he asked, suddenly ravenous.

She nodded. He turned to start walking, but people were in his way, surging toward his parents. As if they all at once decided this was the time to talk to them, though August already knew that Duke would be uncomfortable, and his mom would be embarrassed.

He didn't know why grown-ups did this when they didn't have to. But Duke said that some things people did because it was the right thing to do, and August put that thought in a special place in his head. A place for memories that he wanted to always remember.

"Come one." He grabbed Elle's hand to steer her around them.

She skipped by his side, and he looked over at her. "You should be a dancer."

"I'd rather be a karate fighter," she said. "I could kill the bad guys."

He laughed, and that tightness he'd felt earlier was gone, and his throat was open. He saw a couple of boys in his class looking at him, and he knew when he got to school that they would tease him for holding hands with a girl, but he didn't care.

It wasn't like he was going to see her for a long while. She was going back to Madison with her mom, and he was staying here with his mom.

There were only a few pieces of cake left by the table, and they both grabbed one and ate. She didn't finish hers, though. Instead, she wrapped it in a napkin, then whispered, "Let's give some to the dogs."

He scratched his head. "You're going to get me into trouble."

Laughing, she turned and half skipped and half walked toward the door to the hallway. He recalled that she knew the place almost as well as he did.

At the door, something made him look behind him, and he saw Mrs. Pascal, a blond lady who used to be married to the brother of Duke's first wife, staring past him at Elle.

Frowning, he turned and hurried after Elle.

He had an odd feeling, like spiders crawling inside his belly, that he shouldn't leave her alone.

Ten

That girl! Sylvia watched the girl leave, and she seemed to be half dancing like a fairy, the boy hurrying after her.

Sylvia couldn't remember her name, but she recognized Jenny Styles's daughter. Jenny and her daughter had left town more than two years ago. She knew that Jenny wasn't getting a lot of money to support herself and her daughter, but looking at the girl, she wouldn't have guessed they were in any financial straits.

Yesterday, as Sylvia had stood in the gun club, she'd been in a dark, unhappy place.

It seemed that she'd been stuck in that place for too long.

But today she saw the joy in the child's face, as if sunlight were spilling out of her pores. It touched something inside her. The joy on the girl's face had been like...well, like seeing a face of God.

Though Sylvia frequently went to church, she had never really believed in God.

A question stopped her. Froze her.

What if she were wrong?

What if the way she'd looked at life all of these years, like it was a never-ending to-do list, was the wrong way to live?

What if instead of looking at all the unhappiness in life, she should be like the girl—looking for the happiness?

The question lingering in her mind, she shivered and her insides shook like a leaf swirling in a tornado. Clenching her mouth, she held back a cry.

What if maybe...just maybe...she could find some of that joy inside herself? The same joy that the girl felt?

She was so tired of being bitter and discontented. So tired of judging other people. Knowing that they were doing things wrong but never able to fix them.

So tired of feeling hatred that so often seemed like a poison inside of her. And it wasn't a small poison. It kept growing and growing. Bigger and fatter.

She didn't want to be that hateful person anymore.

"Hey, you okay?"

A hand draped over her shoulder. She blinked and stared at John Norman. His wide mouth twisted. "Looks like the big fish got away from you."

Immediately, her anger swirled up.

Immediately, she wanted to kick him in his balls.

She realized she'd never liked him.

He was not a good person.

And neither was she.

His eyebrows rose, and she saw they were scraggly and that he had nose hair.

If he'd been a nice person, a jolly person, she wouldn't mind the eyebrows that were sticking up. She wouldn't mind the nose hair.

After all, she was thirty-two. She wasn't new and smooth and perfect anymore. Her skin was still tight enough, but she could see the slight changes. She still turned heads, but the turned heads were older now, her youthful glow dimmed. And in her magnifying mirror at home, she could see the tiny beginnings of decay. She was like a peach that was ripe, but she knew if she kept the peach on the counter too long before eating it, it would soon be overripe.

"Sylvia?" John took his hand off her shoulder and stepped back. "Something wrong?"

She clamped her lips together for the second time tonight. This time to stop herself from laughing hysterically.

Maybe she should laugh out loud. Maybe she would do something a little wild. She should go out on the dance floor and show all the moves that she'd never used in public before. Show those teenaged girls that anything they could do, a thirty-two-year-old woman could do ten times better.

The town would be shocked.

She liked that thought.

"I'll get Chuck." He turned away.

She opened her mouth to tell him not to go. But nothing came out. She peered around. She was still inside the room, with people chattering around her. But no one was coming near her. She had friends, but no real friends. No one who loved her except Chuck.

Didn't he?

She glanced over the crowded room, and she spotted John Norman first and then, next to him, her blond-haired son. A sick feeling twisted inside her stomach. John was gesturing toward her, and Chuck was shaking his head.

He didn't want to come by her.

Yes, he was eleven, the age where he preferred his friends over his mother, but bile still pushed up into her throat.

Regrets. That's what it was, that sour taste in her mouth.

She turned and stalked out of the hall, leaving behind the music and the wedding guests and her son, who didn't love her. She'd been on her way to the ladies' room when she'd spotted the girl, and her purse was on her arm. The cloakroom was in the next door, and she found her warm black wool jacket that went with everything.

Chuck already had made plans to stay with friends overnight. He wouldn't miss him. He probably wouldn't notice she was gone.

Feeling like she was sleepwalking, she left. But she wasn't leaving behind the music and the people who didn't like her.

Instead, she was walking toward something. She wasn't sure what it was. All she knew was that it was somewhere different. Toward something new.

The death of her husband hadn't changed her. It had made her bitter. Made her meaner.

But she'd been bitter and mean for a very long time.

She didn't want to be that way anymore.

She wanted to be joyful. Like the redheaded girl.

Was it too late to change?

She opened the door, shivering. She couldn't answer her question. All she knew for sure was that if she kept this up, she'd be miserable for the rest of her life. Maybe she didn't deserve to be happy, but she was sure the hell going to try.

Eleven

Sixteen years later... Almost home.

August came home with an aching heart.

As he headed to the baggage carousel with travelers crowded around it, waiting for their luggage, he spotted a tall man with white hair pointing at him. Duke. August knew his mom must be next to him, blocked by a group of bigger men.

A movement caught his eye, a small woman squeezing between two of the paunchy men.

Elle. Just looking at her determined expression, the same stubbornness he'd seen that first night at her home, made him feel lighter. Made him feel that he was home.

Then she popped through, and his first thought was, *Whoa. Popped* was an appropriate word, considering her bulging belly.

His gaze swept up to her face. She ran toward him, beaming, her normal grace awkward. He blinked out of his stupor and took wide strides toward her.

"Welcome home!" Still smiling, she took a little

jump to grab his shoulders and pull him close, her belly pushing against him.

The baby gave a big kick.

He yelped and jumpcd back.

She laughed. "You fought insurgents, but you're afraid of a little baby kick?"

A few chuckles came from behind them. His face burned. This wasn't the homecoming he'd envisioned.

"Someone should've warned me." He glanced down at her belly.

"Maybe they would have—if it were any of your business."

As more chuckles came, his mom called out, "Augusto!"

Elle stepped back, and he hugged his mom and she hugged him back, holding him tightly. Over the top of his mom's head, he still stared at Elle. He felt as if he'd been sucker-punched in his stomach.

His mom drew back from him, and he turned his attention to her and the happy tears running down her cheeks. She brought her hands up again, holding the sides of his face.

"My boy," she whispered. "My darling boy. My brave soldier."

"Mama." He heard the thickness in his voice, his own tears not far away. But crying was pointless, and he clenched his fingers tightly to stop him thinking about his emotions.

"I wish you were home for good instead of just a few days."

"Soon. Just two more years." Two years. He could do it. He owed it to this country that had accepted him and his mother. Maybe not always gracefully, not until Elle and her mother had picked them off the side of the road. After that, everything had changed.

A hand clapped his shoulder. Duke. The big man clasped his arms around him, and they hugged. Though Duke wasn't much of a talker, August felt his affection.

"Glad you're back home." Duke released him and stepped next to Pilar, putting his arm around her. "I'm eager for you to be home for good. Your mom and I are ready to take it easy."

"What about Chuck?" he asked.

Duke shook his head, and August nodded. This wasn't the time or place to talk about business. Chuck Pascal was Duke's nephew from his first wife. As a teen, August had worked at the resort with Chuck. Chuck was a year older than him. He was reliable and did what he was told. He grinned a lot. The women liked him. August liked him, too. He was a good worker when told what to do but not a take-charge kind of guy.

A scream came from behind August. He snapped around and saw a Marine who had been on his plane, a few rows behind him, getting engulfed by sobbing and blubbering family members, his mother calling the tall Marine "my baby boy" as tears ran down her cheeks.

August's chest welled up, though he had no reason. He was aware that the transition back to civilian life was impossible for some. He still had to go back, but he was lucky to have his tech skills. That's what everyone told him, and he knew it was true. He'd been one of the lucky ones. Never shot at. Never in danger. And so damn happy to be home only his will power kept him from crying happy tears.

Yet there was a ball of sadness inside him.

He'd heard too many stories. Seen too many injured men and women...and sometimes children, dogs, and cats.

As they walked on to the baggage carousel, a slender hand slid around his and squeezed.

He didn't have to look to his side to see the bright hair. Blinking hard, he willed a rush of tears back, and he didn't let go of her hand.

Twelve

Despite a lower backache that had plagued her since waking up this morning—and feeling like a baby whale—Elle was happy. August was home again. Not for good but for *now*. She'd like more than that, but she was grateful he was home for now.

Though it was March and in the low forties, the air felt fresh, invigorating. Right now, life felt good.

For the first hour's drive from Milwaukee to Door County, Pilar kept turning around in the front passenger seat of Duke's Jeep to bombard August with questions that August mostly fobbed off, saying the least words possible. A few times he settled for grunts. And he didn't fall into tears—not like Pilar, who was so happy to see her "baby boy" home.

As Elle listened to them, she alternated looking out the window and trying to catch sight of the greenish-brown grass between patches of melting snow. The first signs of spring sneaking into Wisconsin.

August replied to something Pilar said, and

Elle glanced at him. Not paying attention to the words, just appreciating the comforting tone in his voice, the deepness, the maturity. The view, too. August's golden skin, black hair, and chiseled cheekbones and jaw.

He was twenty-six, and he seemed more of a man than the last time she saw him. More mature. He still wasn't done with the military. Pilar had told her he was taking classes at night, aiming for a major in business, while he was stationed in different places. It took time. Pilar's biggest complaint was that he was too busy to meet women.

Elle had remained silent. She had hoped he would take classes at Madison. Instead, he'd taken the military route. A longer, harder route, though not as costly. A route that had taken him away from her.

And she knew that Duke would've paid for his schooling, but August was so stubborn...

After that, she'd missed him on his few visits home, busy with her own classes and keeping her grades high enough to earn scholarships, and then starting her dissertation before life got in the way.

The baby kicked. Her hand settled on her stomach. So huge. If she weren't in the car with the others, she would sing to the baby or tell it a story.

On the other side of the backseat, August leaned toward her. She blinked and looked at the seat before her. Pilar was facing the road now, and either she or Duke had turned on a radio station that was playing an old Norah Jones song.

The baby stopped kicking, and Elle breathed easier. Norah Jones's voice made her want to feel slow and sexy and silky. In another couple months maybe—but by then August would be somewhere else again.

"So, it is going to pop out before we get home?" he asked.

She laughed, then clenched her pelvic muscles, turning to look at him. "If you make me laugh again without warning me, I'm going to pee."

He chuckled. "Too much information."

"The baby's not due for three weeks." Three weeks had never felt so far away.

"What about the father?"

She made a face. "I don't want to talk about him."

"Is he giving you any trouble? If he is—"

"I didn't have to use my karate chops on him."

The corners of his mouth turned up. "Anyone else?"

"I used a few moves once in a club."

He chuckled. "You took someone down?"

The memory made her feel like Super Girl instead of Stuffed and Clumsy Girl. "I did. It felt good, too." She turned toward him. "Did you use it?"

He shrugged. "I only took one year. I was more interested in learning how to sail and fish."

"You're such a guy."

"And you're changing the subject. Something's not right. It's the father, isn't it?"

She looked away from him. "I told you, it's okay. I'm handling him."

Marc Cohn's soulful voice singing "Walking

in Memphis" poured out of the Jeep's sound system.

"You shouldn't have to handle him." His voice roughened, and goose bumps popped up on her arms.

"He won't hurt me. Let's change the subject."

August didn't reply, and they listened to Marc Cohn singing about walking on Beale Street and meeting Reverend Green, his rich voice and hopeful message washing over her like a benediction.

She relaxed. Between Marc Cohn and August, she felt better. As if everything would be okay.

Someday she would take her baby to Beale Street and remember this moment.

"If the father does hurt you..." August left the sentence unfinished.

She snapped around and glared at him. So much for her soothing thoughts. "You won't let it go, will you? Don't worry about him. He's a professor at the university, and hurting me would cost him his career. He won't do that."

"Instead, he's hurting you emotionally."

"He's not. He's a psychology professor, and he thinks he knows how to mess with minds. But I know his tricks, and it's not working." She kept her voice low, aware of his parents in the front seat. "He already has a new girlfriend. He won't be a problem."

"Okay, but if you need help..."

"I won't." She exhaled. "But if he does, I'll tell him to watch out for my Marine friend."

He laughed, and she leaned back and let herself feel happy again. After all, he was home for the next two weeks, safe and sitting next to her. "You're happy to be home?"

"More than you know." He didn't talk for another minute, and when he did, his voice was low. "I wish my leave was longer so I could be here for the baby's birth."

She swallowed. She didn't want him to say these things. It made her feel...squirmy inside. And she was too pregnant to feel that way. She'd had a crush on August since Pilar's and Duke's wedding, when she was only eight.

It wasn't just that he looked so good. It was his character. So upright and honest yet so...well, *hot*.

Okay, that was his body. But having a great character was hot, too.

She sighed. If she hadn't been pregnant, she might have done something about her crush...

Or if he'd been home in Trouble Bay in the last few years on the same days she'd been home in Trouble Bay...

Too many *ifs*.

And soon she was going to be a mom.

She put her hand over her belly. *You are going to be loved.*

There was a movement, as if the baby was agreeing.

Then there was an instant of pain.

Oh no. Oh no.

It couldn't be a contraction. Maybe a stomachache. She'd been hungry this morning. She'd driven to the resort yesterday, deciding to drive in to see August with his mother and stepfather. No, *father*. Duke had adopted August after the wedding. And Pilar had invited her to eat breakfast with her and Duke in the chalet where they lived, on a plot of land next to the resort. A short walk away was August's two-bedroom chalet where she'd stayed last night.

She'd been pleased to use it. To be part of this family. And she'd enjoyed eating breakfast with Pilar and Duke this morning in their bright kitchen. An omelet with salsa, Monterey Jack cheese, diced onions, green pepper, and mushrooms.

Pilar had spoiled her. After breakfast, there had been a bowl of fruit. Strawberries, blueberries, and blackberries. And then there'd been a square of seventy-percent dark chocolate. Dark chocolate was getting her through her pregnancy.

It was possible she might have eaten too much.

Beneath her hand, her stomach moved again.

"You're not having the baby now, are you?" August looked at her stomach as if he feared an alien would pop out.

"The baby's getting frisky." She breathed a sigh of relief that it wasn't anything worse. "Want to feel?"

When he didn't reply, she looked up. He was still staring at her belly, his complexion a shade paler.

She took his hand and put it over her belly. He had long fingers, and if she hadn't been pregnant, his fingers might have spread from one side of her pelvic bone to the other. But as it was, she—

Another kick came, and his gaze snapped up to meet her eyes.

She laughed at the surprise on his face. "Now,

that's a—" A sudden pain ripped through her, and she bent forward, sucking her breath in so that it hissed.

Not now. Please, not now.

"You're having contractions," he said.

In the front seat, Duke said, "Tell me you're not having the baby now."

"I'm not having it now." She sat up, her breath back.

"It's her second contraction in just a few minutes," August said.

"The first baby doesn't come fast." She raised her voice. "Isn't that right, Aunt Pilar?"

Pilar turned as far as she could, craning her head around. "Babies come when babies come. They don't punch a time clock."

Elle was getting hot. "I don't want to have the baby in Milwaukee. I want to have it at home."

"Madison?" August asked.

"Not Madison." She was sweating now. Hot. Was the car heater on too high? "Door County."

As August stared at her for a long moment, she felt the car speed up.

She turned her gaze forward, forcing herself to take long inhales and exhales. Her baby was in danger of coming out of her body too soon. Three weeks early.

She wished there were some way to hold it back.

August put his hand back on her stomach, then bent sideways until his face was only a few inches from her burgeoning belly.

"You're going to be okay," he murmured. "Everything is going to be all right." He lifted his head. "Do you have a name for the baby?"

"Harper. She's a girl."

"Good name."

Leaning back, she closed her eyes. Her stomach seemed to be settled. Maybe she'd be okay. Maybe she'd make it. August put his hand over hers and laced their fingers together. She kept her eyes closed as hot tears warmed them.

He was probably holding her hand because he knew she'd clench his fingers when she had another contraction.

"Why Door County?" he asked. "The Green Bay hospital is bigger. If anything happens—"

"Nothing is going to happen to the baby." She heard her sharp tone as she opened her eyes and glared at him. "*Nothing.* And I'm going to have it in Door County because it's home."

There was only the sound of music as the Jeep surged ahead.

"Isn't Madison your home?"

She frowned. Since she'd been six, she'd visited Trouble Bay occasionally, but she lived in Madison. There was so much to do, with great people and restaurants and entertainment year-round.

So why was she so set on having the baby in Door County?

He smiled, but his eyes were serious. "I get it. Door County is my home, too."

Another contraction ripped through her.

She looked down at her stomach.

Not yet, baby. Not yet.

Thirteen

Just as they neared the first Green Bay exit, Elle's breath sucked in loudly.

"What is it?" August asked.

"Nothing." Her voice was strangled.

"It's something. I can tell."

"Since when have you been an expert on me?" She spoke through gritted teeth and glared at him.

Since the day she'd convinced her mother to stop and pick up the mother and son standing on the roadside in winter, he thought. That's when he'd first started to be an expert on her.

Duke put his turn signals on and steered into the outer lane. "We have to go to the hospital. I can't take the chance that the baby will be born in the car."

"The last contraction was ten minutes ago. I might have hours before the baby is ready to pop out." Her face was flushed and sweaty-looking, her freckles orange.

This was not her best look, but August supposed he wouldn't be looking his best if he were about to push out a baby. He'd never thought about it before, but what men did to women wasn't good for them. She was looking sick and nervous, and he was feeling a little sick himself. Grateful, too. Glad right now that he was a guy.

"Is she all right?" Duke asked.

"I don't know." August's mom gestured with her hands, her shoulders up in a shrug. "Sometimes babies come early. Sometimes they don't. I told you before that babies have their own time clock."

"That's not much help," Duke said.

She shrugged again. "If the baby comes in your car, I will help birth it."

"I'll trust you, Aunt Pilar," Elle said. "Uncle Duke, please keep driving. It won't take long to get to the hospital. Babies aren't usually in a hurry. If the contractions are ten minutes apart, I could be in labor for *hours*. Please, Uncle Duke. *Please*."

"If you say so." Duke sighed, then the car sped past the exit, and August repressed a moan.

Elle's laugh was shaky. "Love you, Uncle Duke."

August held her hand and reminded himself to breathe. She was going to have a baby. But the funny thing was that it felt as if *they* were going to have a baby. "Do you want me to call the father now?"

"Do you want me to kick you in your balls?"

He laughed. That was the Elle he loved.

Like a sister. *Almost* a sister.

How could he not love her? If not for her, he didn't know what would have happened to him all those years ago. Or what would have happened to his mother.

She might still be cleaning rooms at cheap motels.

And him... He didn't know, but he had the feeling his future would have been harder.

Elle's hand cupped the left side of his face. "What is it?" she whispered.

He shook his head, using his will-power to force back the itch of tears.

"You look...sick," she said. "Good thing you're not an obstetrician."

"Yeah, good thing." He put his hand over hers on the side of his face, holding it there because it felt good. "Don't worry. I've got your back."

"I hate to break it to you," she said, her voice husky, "but it's not my back that will need medical help."

In the front seat, his mom and Duke laughed. He exhaled. If they could laugh, it was going to be okay.

"I've got you," he said. "I've got you good. No matter what."

It would take less than an hour to get to the Door County Hospital in Sturgeon Bay. A lot could happen in an hour.

"I know you'll take care of me," she said. "Whatever you do, you're good at. No, not good." Her eyes didn't leave his, as if she drew strength from him. "You excel."

"Not everything. Not delivering babies. We should turn back. If the baby comes before we get there... I don't know."

She grimaced. "August, don't turn into a wuss now."

He fought an urge to laugh wildly. "You're

headstrong and stubborn and bossy."

She made a face at him. "Don't forget to add *short* to that list. And a redhead. We all have our faults."

Her breath hissed in again. Pain rippling through her. He felt it a second before she gripped his hands. His stomach clenched, and he felt hot and uncomfortable, as if he were the one in pain.

"Short isn't a fault," he said. "It's a height. And having babies isn't for wusses."

Her eyelids flickered down. "You think we're almost there yet?"

"Yes."

She smiled, her eyes still closed. "Liar. Talk to me. Tell me why you enlisted. You didn't have to."

"He's too independent," Duke said from the front seat, a growl in his voice. "I would've paid for his education. Talk about stubborn. There are two stubborn donkeys in that backseat."

August smiled, a rush of love for his parents. Maybe Duke wasn't his real dad, but he hadn't seen his real father since he was three. In every way that mattered, Duke was the dad of his heart.

"I didn't go to the Marines just for that, Dad. I joined because my mom came to this country as a young girl. And even when we lived in the worst part of Chicago, she told me that we were lucky to be citizens of this great country."

Elle sniffed. "That's so...wonderful."

He looked down at her face that was pale now except for the blotches on her cheeks. He set his lips, not ready to tell her that the other reason he joined the Marines was because of her and her mother. The woman and the girl who'd saved them after their Marine husband and father had been killed.

Combined with his mother's gratitude, it had made him want to pay them back. As a bonus, he was getting an education, most of it paid for.

Only two more years, and he'd be home for good.

"I'm not sweet." He smiled down at her. "I'm a Marine, and we're tough."

"That means you'll be in the delivery room with me, right?" Her tone was light, but her eyes didn't leave his, her expression anxious.

"Of course, I will. Whatever happens. I can take it."

Fourteen

So tiny. Watching the baby's birth had been like watching the creation of one of the marvels of the world. August couldn't talk as the nurse put the baby on Elle's chest and said, "Say hello to mama."

"Hi, baby. Hello, sweetheart. Welcome to the world." Elle was half crying, her voice wobbly, her hair damp from sweat, and her face blotchy.

She'd never looked more beautiful to August as the nurse wiped the baby and Elle cooed to it in weepy tones.

"She's so beautiful." Elle glanced at August, then her gaze swept back to the baby. "You're beautiful, beautiful. My beautiful girl."

"A redhead," the nurse said as she somehow unhooked the sweat-stained hospital gown and murmured something to Elle, who said, "Yes."

The nurse unsnapped the gown at Elle's shoulders, and the doctors were doing something below Elle's waist that August didn't want to watch, even if he could take his eyes off the baby. He didn't know if Elle still wanted him here, but she had no trouble being vocal about what she didn't want, and that was for him to leave. And there was nothing erotic about this baring of her breast so the baby could suckle. There was only just...something beautiful.

The wonder of it squeezed his chest and took his breath. It was amazing. The birth of a baby. A person. This little girl baby with a head too big for her body and already covered with damp, red curls, her face squished slightly so she looked like a small child's awkward drawing.

"Can I touch?" he asked in a hushed voice.

"Yes," Elle said. "Isn't she beautiful?"

He bent forward, too choked to answer. He carefully touched the side of the baby's face, and she made a sound in her throat. Not a cry. Just a noise to say, *I'm here. I'm here.*

"Yes, you are here," he whispered, rubbing his finger along her chin. "How are you, sweet baby?"

And then he did something that he hadn't done during his tour in Afghanistan. That he hadn't done since the night in Chicago that his friend was killed.

He silently cried. But this wasn't from grief or anger or pain. This was from happiness.

Fifteen

Sylvia had been careful. Very careful. She'd driven to Green Bay mid-morning and rented a white sedan, then drove back to Door County, wearing sunglasses and a brown wig, taking the lake road and turning onto the stone driveway that led to Ann Marie Hodge's cabin. Everyone in Trouble Bay knew that Ann Marie was in Las Vegas and wouldn't return until the beginning of tourist season, when she would open her shop for local artists.

Sylvia *liked* Ann Marie. Liked her sharp tongue and her good taste in art. But Ann Marie was far away now, and no one would blame her for what Sylvia was about to do.

It wasn't likely anyone would even find out. The closest neighbors were a newly married couple from Milwaukee and their adopted son. They were renting the house next door until they found a place they wanted to buy. The woman's father was a wood sculptor who lived down the road. Bill Quinn. He'd asked Sylvia out about five years ago, but she'd turned him down. He was handsome in a rough way, but he wasn't her type. He used axes and chainsaws for his sculptures, and they sold very well...

She stopped her thoughts, realizing that she was trying to avoid thinking about what she was about to do. This wasn't like her. Of course, what she was about to do wasn't going to be pleasant, but she was correcting a wrong. Her anger was eating at her. And, really, the fact that Paul Finney had agreed to meet her here confirmed that he was incompetent as well as a liar. If he'd been a halfway decent insurance agent, he would have known his area. He would have been aware that Ann Marie wasn't around.

Better yet, if he'd been a halfway decent human with an ounce of compassion—and ditto on the insurance company he worked for—none of this would be necessary.

Instead, he and his insurance company had sworn she hadn't made the payment on time. She'd driven to Paul's office, two towns over, and given him the check the week before it was due. A week and a half before the storm had whipped through town and lightning had struck her house, slicing through the roof like it was soft butter and striking the dry wood of the attic floor, igniting a fire while she and her guests slept. The fire alarm had woken her guests as smoke filled the rooms on the third floor and the ceiling was compromised.

A terrible, terrible night.

She counted herself lucky that no one had been hurt and no one had died.

But after that, her luck had run out...

Though she had the payment receipt, the

insurance company had claimed that the receipt was doctored, and they were ready to bring a handwriting expert to court to prove it.

The lawyer she'd consulted had said she could take it to court, but he couldn't promise they would win. And she couldn't afford to pay him large amounts on that small chance.

She was screwed.

That was when she'd known what she needed to do.

Not right then. Other things came first.

She'd had to get a second mortgage for her house. She'd lost four months of income while repairs had been made.

Chuck had dropped out of college.

He hadn't been sorry. He should have graduated three or four years ago. Sure, he worked part-time, but so did other students, and they handled more classes. She finally admitted that he didn't have an academic mind.

Perhaps the pitying whispers she'd overheard were true, and she was throwing her money away...but he was all she had. She'd wanted so badly for him to do well in life, she'd been ready to push him through, whether he wanted it or not.

But now, he insisted she couldn't afford it. Ignoring her protests, he was working full-time at Duke's resort, and he seemed to enjoy it. He liked people, and they liked him. Certainly, she preferred that he worked for Duke instead of working at one of the taverns.

Still, she worried. She knew her son. She loved him, but she knew him. He had a good heart but no ambition. He was too much like her late, unlamented husband.

She'd wanted more for Chuck, but now her hopes were smashed like a bug that had been stepped on. Though Chuck had a good heart, she worried that he could still go down the road that his father had taken. That slippery road to drink and drugs and slutty women.

All because of the greedy insurance company and the incompetent, lying agent.

Paul Finney had to pay.

She'd waited, letting the days pass by, the weeks, and then the months. Not saying anything, not mentioning his name, waiting for the right time to act.

Now was the right time.

Ann Marie's cabin was situated at the end of a driveway that must've been about a quarter mile long. She only had a small patch of grass, with woods on either side of the cabin and the harbor behind her. There were still broken slabs of ice on the bay, and Sylvia couldn't see any ships, recreational or otherwise.

She stopped the car, took off her brown wig, then combed her blond hair before stepping out of the car and breathing in the cleanness of the cold air, the sun bright, the sky blue. No one in sight.

Perfect. No one would see her. No one would know.

The sound of a car engine on the road made her sigh. She wasn't ready to leave this peaceful place. Since Duke's wedding to Pilar—sixteen years now—she'd changed. She had embraced joy—at least as much as anyone with her judgmental temperament could change.

When she was with other people, she still saw their faults, but she'd learned to rein in her disapproval, and she tried to look for the good in them. Usually she could find *something* to admire. After all, she was well aware that she wasn't perfect. She could hold grudges. And sometimes she might be, well, revengeful.

Acknowledgment of her own shortcomings had been the key to her transformation. That and her quest for joy. Though she hadn't reached nirvana, she'd found stretches of happiness and contentment. And she had friends now. People who *liked* her. Before this change of heart, people were *afraid* of her. When they had seen her, smiles had frozen on their faces. Now, they gave her real smiles. They were *happy* to see her.

Her life wasn't perfect, but it wasn't a bad life.

At least it hadn't been until the lightning strike had taken off the third floor of her house and had caused more than six figures of damage, bringing her from comfortable to deeply in debt.

The sound of tires on gravel caught her attention.

It reminded her of driving into the nightclub parking lot.

That had been the night she'd said good-bye to Charley for good.

He'd been a liar and a cheater.

The night before, he'd told her he was going to leave her. All his money was gone, and he was going to ask for half of the home that her great-great-grandparents had built in the early 1900s and half of the money that had been left in her trust fund.

She'd begged him not to do that. To leave it intact for their son.

He'd laughed at her protests. He didn't care about Chuck. He didn't care about her.

He'd had to pay.

Now it was the lying, cheating insurance agent's time to pay.

The car stopped about ten yards behind her car. She didn't turn around yet. Still looking out at the waterway, the blue horizon, and the ragged white clouds. It truly was beautiful.

"Mrs. Hodge," a call came, and she recognized Paul's eager-to-please voice. At least, eager-to-please when he was taking your money. Smooth and impersonal when he was lying his chubby ass off.

She still didn't turn, letting him come closer. Only when she heard the crunch of his footsteps a couple feet away did she turn.

He took a step back, his surprise reflected on his almost handsome face with the light blue eyes and light brown hair. He wore gray slacks and a black cashmere-blend overcoat. She could see a few inches above the collar that he had on a dark blue shirt and a gray tie. Nothing cheap, but of course, he could afford it. The insurance company he worked for had probably given him a bonus for not sending in her claim and saving them money.

"Um, Sylvia." He looked around at the house, his Adam's apple bobbing. "I didn't expect to see you here."

"I know." She slid her hand into her purse, and she smiled. Like a purring cat, she thought as she curled her fingers around her late father's unregistered Berctta.

It wasn't the gun she'd used to kill Charley. That had been Charley's gun, a Glock 19. At the time, she'd liked the irony that he'd been killed by his own gun.

She'd made the decision out of bitterness, but she still liked the irony.

He glanced around, his own hand in his overcoat pocket.

Her grip on the Beretta firm and steady, she slid it out of her purse. "Remove your hand from your pocket."

His eyes widened.

"Now." Her sharp voice sliced through the chill air.

"You wouldn't."

"One." She raised the gun, then aimed the muzzle at his chest. "Two."

He pulled his hand out, and she saw that it was shaking. "Sylvia, you really don't want to do this."

"Actually, you're wrong. I do want to do this." She lowered the gun toward his left thigh and put her other hand around her hand holding the gun to steady it.

"Sylvia, I'm sorry. I didn't—"

She pulled the trigger.

He screamed. "You *shot* me!"

"And you cheated me." This time she shot at his shoulder.

He screamed again.

She made a face. Her aim had been a little off this time, and the bullet had entered his upper arm. Too much adrenaline surging through her had caused the wrong angle.

"You really, really shouldn't lie and cheat," she said, and was pleased that her voice didn't shake.

A whimper came out of his mouth. "I'm sorry. I'm sorry. I won't do it again. I promise."

She stepped toward him, the gun aimed at his chest again. "Paul, you've already proven yourself to be a liar. A man without a conscience. You really expect me to believe your promises?"

"Please, please, please. You can't do this."

She stepped toward him, unsmiling. "Sure, I can." She heard the chirpiness in her voice. "And you know what? I'm just doing to you what you were doing to me. I don't feel a bit guilty."

He shook his head, his eyes wide as he scuttled back. His wounded leg buckled, and he cried out. "Don't do this, Sylvia. Don't do—"

She aimed at his left chest and shot. The bullet flew straight through at the target point. He made a funny noise and jerked back. Staring at her, though she knew he saw nothing as he toppled to his left.

Already dead.

Sixteen

The nurse took the baby away for tests, and Elle watched until the door closed behind her. Only then did she turn to August, his chair drawn up to her bed. Pilar and Duke had headed to the cafeteria, and it was just her and August in the hospital room.

August's forehead was furrowed, and she could practically see his brain cells whirling.

"You'll have a great story when you return to the base," she said. "You're having an interesting leave."

"Make it more interesting." He leaned closer over the hospital bed. "Marry me."

"*What?*" She pushed up slightly but winced and dropped back on her pillows. No sudden moves for her just yet. "Where did that come from?"

"The baby needs a daddy."

"August, no." Tears stung Elle's eyes, and she didn't want to cry today.

"I know the father's not going to be there for you and Harper. My mom told me everything while the nurses were taking off your clothes. I know he's an asshole who lied about being separated from his wife. And he has a child with another woman besides his two with his wife. I know—"

"Too much." She held out her hand to stop him. She didn't want this to be about Harper's father. She wanted this to be about the baby. About Harper. She wanted her birth to be joyous, and to hell with the baby daddy.

She took a deep breath because she had worried when they'd rushed to the hospital three weeks early. But Harper was two ounces over five pounds, and everything seemed to be working properly. Though she was having more tests, the nurses were cheerful, and they hadn't given off any concerned vibrations.

Harper had even attempted to suckle Elle's breast already—an odd feeling—with August sitting there, watching, and it hadn't felt erotic or like something she'd had to hide. It had just felt *right*. After all, that was the function that breasts were made for.

"Listen." She put her hand on his on the bed sheet next to her. "Harper and I are going to be fine. You didn't have a father for a few years, and you're doing well. Same here."

"I'm not taking anything away from my mom. My dad was never home a lot, but after he left, I missed having a dad sometimes." His eyes never left hers. "And when we lived with Duke, he felt like a dad right from the first week."

She fought an urge to hug him and reminded herself that he wasn't that little boy anymore.

And she wasn't the little girl with the crush on the boy.

"Uncle Duke is great," she said. "When Mom and I lived in Trouble Bay, he used to help us out when we needed him. Not financial help, because my mom said we had enough, but she'd call him when something in the house or the car broke. He always came. I missed him when we moved to Madison. I know my mom missed him, too."

"And your dad," he said.

She sighed. "He died so young. My mom still talks about him. He sounds like a great man, but..." She sighed and pulled her hand back from his. "I hardly remember him. And it didn't take long after we moved to Madison for Mom to make great women friends who were always there for us." She shrugged. "When you're young, the gender of the people who care for you doesn't matter. All that mattered was that it wasn't just me and my mom. There was a support system. Harper is going to have that, too."

"Will she?" His gaze penetrated, not letting her look away. Not letting her lie. Or even stretch the truth.

"Most of my friends are single." Actively single. She was the first to have a baby. "I don't know, but we'll work it out."

"You were so insistent on having the baby here." A corner of his lips curved up. "You said you wanted to have it close to home. You do consider Trouble Bay to be home."

She frowned. Why did he have to dig so deep? She'd just had a baby. She wanted to sleep.

"It's the home of my heart." She attempted to smile. "We're getting too serious. I've just had a big shock to my body. And to my emotions. I feel"—she laughed but there was a sob in it—"as if I've been bombed by a tsunami of love." The tears were coming, and she scrunched her face to stop them. "I love that little squishy face."

"A bulldog face." His voice was soft. "The prettiest bulldog face I've seen."

She put her hand over her left breast. "When I look at her, I feel my heart grow bigger."

"Do you want to call her father?" August asked.

She grabbed a tissue and blew her nose. The small movement hurt her down below. Sheesh. Having babies wasn't for sissies.

Maybe that's why women had them instead of men.

"Not now. Later. I doubt Warren will spend much time with her."

"He sounds like an ass," August said. "Someone should report him to the college administrators."

"I wasn't his student when it happened. Besides, if he's fired, he won't be able to pay support for any of his children."

"That's his problem."

"No, it will be our problem."

He put his hand over hers. "You don't have to worry. I'll be deployed soon, but I can send you money. Dad will let you stay in one of the—"

"Don't." Her voice was thickening, and she pulled her hand from his. "I told you, I'll be fine on my own. When are Uncle Duke and Aunt Pilar coming back?"

"When they finish eating lunch."

A suspicion burrowed into her mind. "You asked them to leave, didn't you?"

"What if I did? I owe you, Elle." He looked her straight in her eyes.

She pushed up on her elbows, wincing with discomfort at the small movement. "You owe me nothing." She bit the next words out. "Not. A. Thing."

"You don't have to get mad."

"August, with every word you say to me, I'm getting angrier." She lay back on the double pillows. "Your mom and dad already invited me to stay at the resort for as long as I want. I'm still getting my scholarship and living expenses while I write my dissertation. In two weeks, you have to go back to the base, or...whatever."

"I'm returning to Afghanistan," he said, his voice soft.

She closed her eyes. She'd hated it the last time he'd been deployed. Her dad had died in a country far away. She didn't want a repeat.

"I wish I could stay here to help you," he said.

"I'll be okay. Your mother, my mother, and a lot of mothers have raised their children without a man. Probably women have been doing this since there were mothers and babies."

"You make it sound like women don't need men."

"We don't." She made herself smile at him. He was *trying* to help. "But sometimes we want them."

His face tensed. His eyes flashed. "Want me, Elle." He leaned over her. "*Want* me."

Her breath sucked in, then she reached up and cupped her hand over the side of his face. He looked good. So good. His face so lean and golden. Those cheekbones and his chin. The brown eyes, like dark chocolate with lighter caramel flecks. And his lashes. Thick and black and long. Girls would kill for his lashes.

And then there was his body. Yum. Yum. In fact, if she wrote a book about a character who looked like him, she would call him Mr. YumYum.

"My darling friend, I do want you." It would be so easy to say yes. And so wrong. She forced a smile. "You're pretty hot, you know."

He groaned.

She hiccupped a laugh. "Don't you dare make me laugh. You know it will hurt. I just pushed a five-pound baby out of my vagina."

He snorted, then curved his long fingers over the hand still on his cheek, drawing it down to the bed, just holding her hand and smiling at her.

"I could love you," he said.

Could? He *could* love her.

She shook her head. The minute she'd seen him at the airport this morning, her heart had lit up, giving her a message: *Him. All along it's been him.*

Right. That was her pregnancy brain talking. Looking for a man worthy of taking care of her baby and herself.

"Don't," she said, not trusting that brain and those thoughts. "Just don't."

The door opened, and she heard Pilar's voice and jerked her hand away from his. She didn't want Pilar and Duke to get the wrong idea.

"I'm going to be okay," she said to him, her voice low.

He sat up. "I'm putting you down as my

beneficiary. If anything happens to me, you'll get the money."

"August!" she said. "I can't let you do that."

"What a great idea." Pilar clapped her hands together. She stepped forward and put her hand on his shoulder. "But be careful. I don't want anything to happen to you."

"I don't plan on it, but if it does—"

Elle closed her eyes and wished her mom were here. But Jenny was at a conference in Minnesota and planned on leaving right after breakfast tomorrow morning and driving to the hospital.

Really, Elle thought, she had so many people who wanted to take care of her and the baby. She knew Harper was going to be just fine. No, not *fine*. She was going to be *wonderful*.

"What are you thinking?" August asked in a low voice.

She opened her eyes. "When you go back to...well, wherever you're going...will you do me a favor?"

"What?"

"Don't die."

He smiled slowly. "I promise."

"Good." She wanted to kiss him. A sweet kiss, because she certainly wasn't feeling passionate or horny right now. Just a kiss that said *I care. Don't get killed because I care.* "We're going to do just fine."

Uncle Duke and Aunt Pilar left ten minutes later, but August lingered, telling them to go ahead, and he'd meet them in the car.

"I just want to tell you," he looked down at her.

"You said I don't owe you anything, but you're wrong. I owe you everything."

She pressed back against the pillows, shrinking a little inside.

He didn't want her after all.

"If not for you and your mom picking me and my mom up all those years ago, I don't know what would've happened to us."

She still didn't say anything.

He bent to kiss her.

She turned her head, his lips brushing her cheek.

"Elle, what's wrong? What did—"

"I'm tired. Very tired." She closed her eyes. "Take care of yourself."

For another moment, she felt him watching her as she kept her eyes closed and her breaths even. Finally he opened the door and left.

She still kept her eyes closed.

Everything is going to be all right, she told herself. *Everything is going to be all right.* Her eyes closed, and she took a deep breath. *Everything is going to be all right.*

If she said it enough times, she might begin to believe it.

Seventeen

It was harder than Sylvia had thought. Leaving his body where it was for now, she took Paul's keys and drove his car to another house about a mile away that she knew would be empty until fall. She was shaking on the inside but not the outside.

None of this was like her. But she had to take care of all these details. Paul had probably typed Ann Marie's address on his computer or had written it on an appointment sheet. With no car and no body, the police might think he had never been there, and Sylvia didn't have to involve Ann Marie or cause her any inconvenience.

That was the easy part. She began her trek back to the scene of the murder. Twice she heard a car coming and slipped off the road and hid behind a tree, giving thanks for the many trees along the road as her heart thumped madly.

Back at Ann Marie's place, she changed her leather gloves for latex gloves, then took off Paul's clothes, stuffed him into two extra large garbage bags, rolled him onto a blanket then dragged him to the rental car. Gritting her teeth, she hauled up his top half into the trunk, then hoisted up his lower half. Leaning over his body, she panted, her arms shaky and heat prickling beneath her armpits despite the cold.

After a moment, she stepped back, stuffed his clothes and personal items in a garbage bag. When she drove to Green Bay to return the rental, she would put them in a trash container.

For the final destination to complete her task, she put on the wig again and a pair of rubber boots, then drove to one last empty cabin another two miles away. Far enough away that no one would connect the dots. There, she dragged his body out of the car then to the side of the lake. Huffing, she opened the garbage bag that covered his torso.

Fighting her distaste, she used an old steak knife to puncture his chest and belly more than a half dozen times before dropping it into a tangle of brown grass and weeds. By then her hands were shaking, but she didn't let that stop her. She shoved heavy rocks inside the bag, then dragged the bag with the rocks and the body to the shoreline where it dipped into the water. Her breaths heaving, she gave the body in the bag a great push and it rolled downward.

Her teeth clamped together to keep them from chattering, she straightened and watched the body disappear under the blue-green waters. Her arm and leg muscles ached from dragging the body to the bay, and her rubber boots were muddy. But it was done.

She turned away from the bay. She felt...relieved that it was over. Not euphoric. Not thrilled. Not wanting to break into giggles or dance a jig. She wasn't a monster. She was just a woman who had righted a wrong.

She went to pick up the steak knife, wiping the blood on the brown grass, before she headed to the car.

The knife would be thrown in a trash garbage container in Green Bay, too.

At the car, she took off the rubber gloves and boots, then she put on her own shoes, her own gloves, and put the wig back on. She didn't want anyone traveling down the lake road to identify her driving away in this car. When she sat behind the steering will and started the car engine, she was slightly surprised that her hands had stopped shaking.

It was too bad she couldn't take on the entire insurance company, one board member at a time. But if she did that, she would surely be caught. That wasn't in her game plan. Besides, the corporate office of the insurance company was in a different state, and she'd been inconvenienced enough.

She drove back to Green Bay, dumped the items into different trash bins, returned the car to the rental place, picked up her own car, which she'd left in a grocery store parking lot two blocks over, then drove to her home.

She parked in the four-car garage of the white-painted former inn that had catered to fishermen and loggers and other adventurous men and women in the late nineteenth century. In the mid-twentieth century, it been turned into a residence. When she'd inherited it from her grandmother, she'd turned it back into a bed and breakfast. Six bedrooms that she rented out most of the year—four on the second floor and two luxury suites with whirlpools on the upper floor. And then there was her smaller bedroom on the lower floor, behind the kitchen.

The brochures said it was a Greek revival from the mid-nineteenth century, but she suspected the truth was her ancestors had slapped it together and put it on the only road that ran through the small town so they could gouge an extravagant amount from travelers. Just as she was doing now.

Inside her house, she locked herself in her bedroom, cleaned the Beretta, then put it away in the hidden safe in the closet that had been there before she was born.

That done, she took a shower. As the warm water cascaded down on her, she felt a surge of excitement and had a strong desire to have celebratory sex. Why not? After all, she was forty-eight. Not young anymore, but not old, either. And it would be false modesty not to admit that she was still attractive. Though she credited her genetic makeup, she took care of herself. She walked a lot, always wore sun protection and had never smoked. She doubted she was fertile anymore, but she still had a period every month, like it was Old Faithful.

Stepping out of the shower, she saw her body in the full-length mirror screwed onto the bathroom door. Her body wasn't perfect as it had been when she was younger, but she was still slender, and her stomach didn't pouch out too much. Really, she had a better figure than eighty percent of townswomen thirty and under. She could probably do the pencil trick with her breasts—put a pen or a pencil beneath her breasts and let go—and the pencil would fall to the bathroom floor.

She hadn't slept with a man for over seven years. The last time had been a guest, and he had been wealthy and charming. But he'd left her unsatisfied, as did most men.

They'd parted with an almost chaste kiss and no plans to repeat the evening.

But now...maybe it was adrenaline, though she didn't like to think of herself as *that* kind of a person. One who got a perverse thrill from killing. That was *not* why she'd done it. If that were the case, it would make her reprehensible. And when people were so reprehensible, they should...well, be killed. Nothing more and nothing less.

She looked down. Her hands were shaking again, and she was breathing too fast.

She wrapped the towel around her, stepped into her bedroom, then sat on the side of her bed, her hands curled tightly on her thighs. For minutes, she didn't move except to breathe.

Killing wasn't as impersonal as she'd thought.

She no longer wanted to have sex with any man.

But life went on. Her shoulders were getting chilled, and she still needed to sew new curtains for one of the guest bedrooms. Soon, she would need to start dinner. So she stood and put on her clothes. As she finished pulling on her socks, her phone rang.

Her heart pounded. Her hands shaky again.

Had they found Paul already? It didn't seem possible. She'd researched, and a body in fresh water would be pretty much all gone by six months. The skeletal remains might take a few years, but she thought she would be okay.

God, she hoped so.

In the meantime, let the bastard rot a while.

Taking a deep breath, she walked to her bedside table and picked up the phone.

"Did you hear the news?" Angela Dufort's voice was high and shrill with excitement.

Sylvia stiffened. "What news?"

"Elle Styles had her baby in the hospital here."

"Here?" She shook her head. Maybe it was because of what had happened earlier today, but she didn't understand. She didn't know anything about a pregnancy. She hadn't seen Elle and her mom in the past few years, and the baby thing threw her sideways. The last time she'd seen Elle, she had still looked like a teenager. How could this have happened?

Angela was happy to enlighten her, rambling on for ten minutes, though her only facts were that Elle had had a baby girl, and Duke, Pilar, and Pilar's son were with her. And she didn't have the baby in Trouble Bay, which had no hospital, but the hospital two towns over.

Sylvia finally said she had to go. Hanging up, she thought that today a man had died and a baby had been born. How appropriate.

Her hands were steady now, and she felt surprisingly...good.

And why shouldn't she feel good? It wasn't that

she was evil. She'd righted a wrong, and that wasn't wrong.

The same thing that she'd done with Charley.

And if someone wronged her again, she should do it again.

She got up and gathered her embroidery and then the brownies that she'd made this morning. She was meeting the Trouble Bay Crafters this afternoon, and if she hurried, she wouldn't be late. The other women loved her brownie recipe. She made them from scratch, and even she had to admit they were the best in town. Just as her embroidery was the best in town.

Whatever she did, she liked to be the best at.

Even murder.

For a long time, she'd thought she had to be better than anyone. She'd gotten that from her mother.

But she'd never been *happy*. Not until she'd seen the smile on a small girl's face. The joy that Elle had radiated had made Sylvia want some of that same joy.

In the last sixteen years since Duke and Pilar's wedding, Sylvia had been happier for the most part. But it had been a low-level happiness. She'd never reached the height of the young girl's joy.

She knew why now. She'd been holding herself back. She hadn't been her true self. She didn't have to be good all the time. She didn't have to repress her impulses. She just needed to keep a happy medium. Murder in the afternoon and embroidery at night.

Her joke made her laugh harshly, but there was some truth to it.

After all, she had murdered today. And tonight was embroidery club.

Which reminded her. She had a knitted baby blanket in the closet. Perhaps tomorrow she would drive to the hospital and give it to Elle.

Eighteen

Four years later...

"I love Mommy," Harper sang in the booster seat in the backseat of Elle's car. "I love Sammie. I love..."

Driving along I-94, the afternoon sun still bright and the windows closed to keep out the heat, the air on low, Elle could feel Harper going through all the words in her four-year-old mind to find a word to rhyme with *mommy*.

She was so proud of her daughter for making up rhyming songs.

And she was so sick of hearing her sing rhyming songs. Two hours of this so far.

"Grandmommy!" Harper said loudly. "I love Grandmommy. Do you like my song, Mommy?"

"I love your song, sweetie. And I love you."

"Love you, too, Mommy. I'll sing to you again." As she started singing again, Elle wished for earplugs.

At the same time, she wanted to engrave this in her memory.

Age four was a wonderful age. And a terrifying age. Harper wanted to do *everything*. She was fearless.

Elle's mother said Harper was almost a carbon copy of Elle, but Elle couldn't remember having that much energy. Most of the day, Harper didn't have an off switch—just a few periods of utter exhaustion when she'd fall asleep on the living room rug with her mouth open, her arms and legs sprawled out. Giving Elle a chance to do her own work without interruption. By that time, Elle was usually exhausted and ready for her own nap.

Elle hoped she would find friends with kids in Trouble Bay. At the university, she'd been the only one of her friends with a child. Her mother had helped take care of Harper sometimes, but she'd taken an evil glee out of Elle's exhaustion, saying she'd gone through it, too.

Elle was sure that her mother was exaggerating. She had never been as smart and energetic as Harper.

They drove past Green Bay, and it didn't take long before they reached Sturgeon Bay in Door County, the first community on the bay side of the county, with Lake Michigan on the other.

Immediately, Elle's spirits lifted. Her shoulders relaxed. The windows were open slightly, and she inhaled deeply. The air smelled fresh. A mix of sunlight, grass, and water.

Home. That's what it smelled like.

She smiled.

"Are we almost there, Mommy?" Harper asked. "Are we?"

"Almost."

"Door County is my favorite place in the world!"

Elle laughed and heard the carefree joy in her laugh.

"Why don't we stay forever?" Harper asked. Without waiting for an answer, she banged her fists on the arms of her booster seat. "Stay in Trouble Bay forever. Stay forever and ever and ever."

Elle's breath caught. Forever?

Before, it hadn't been possible. Not at first. Then it hadn't been feasible. But now...

Now she didn't know.

Now she would give Harper the same answer that her mother used to give her. "Stop hitting the arms, Harper. As for whether we'll stay, I'm not sure yet. We'll see."

Twenty minutes later, she parked her car in the back of Uncle Duke's resort in Trouble Bay. Harper had taken off her seat belt and was scrambling out of her seat as Elle opened the backseat door.

"We're here." Harper leapt out of the car and danced on the blacktop. "We're here."

A gray-haired couple reaching the sedan next to them chuckled. "The water's still too cold to swim in," the woman called, opening her car door. "But it's beautiful."

"The golf is always good," the man said.

"We're going to live here!" Harper said.

"Harper!"

"Mommy, you said—"

"We'll see. I said we'll see."

The woman laughed again. "*We'll see* are the

two most dangerous words in the world."

As they got into their car, Harper turned to Elle. "What are the best words?"

"I love you."

She frowned. "I think the best words are that we'll live here forever."

"What about 'Let's get our luggage and then go see Uncle Duke and Aunt Pilar.'"

"And Uncle August." Harper took another hop. "You said he was there when I was born! I want to see him."

"We'll see him." The words spurred Elle to move faster. She hadn't warned them, wanting to surprise August. Ever since she'd heard that August was back for good, she'd felt like there was a revved-up engine inside her that wouldn't calm down or slow down until she saw him again.

Four minutes later, they did see August in the lobby. He wasn't alone. There was a smiling young woman and a handsome blond man behind the reception desk. But clinging to August was a tall, thin woman with dark brown hair.

They were kissing.

Nineteen

"Dr. Styles." August grinned at her as the dark-haired beauty kept one arm slung over his neck, leaning onto him.

Elle kept her gaze on August. It had been four years and three months since she'd seen him.

The day Harper had been born.

The day he'd asked her to marry him, and she'd said no.

And now another woman was hanging on his neck, and she might as well have hung a sign around his neck that shouted HANDS OFF. THIS MAN IS MINE.

The hairs on the back of Elle's neck rose, and a danger signal blasted in her ear, though she knew no one else could hear it. Uncharacteristically shy, Harper clung to her, her arms around her thighs, her face turned into the turquoise skirt of Elle's cotton dress.

"It's a little late," Elle said to August, "but welcome home."

"You're a doctor?" the woman's voice rose with an edge of disbelief.

"Doctor of psychology," Elle said, not taking

offense. The brunette's reaction wasn't uncommon. She knew she looked like she wasn't old enough to drink, though she was twenty-eight now. When she was younger, it bothered her. Now she took it as a compliment. "You look familiar. Lissa Norman, right?"

Lissa's eyebrows rose. "I know you?"

"I used to live here." Elle gestured in the direction of the town. "A long time ago. Don't worry. We weren't besties."

August snorted, and the girl at the reception counter giggled.

Elle turned to his clinging friend. "I'm Elle Styles." She put her hand on Harper's head, feeling the silken curls beneath her palm. "This is Harper, my daughter."

"Oh, yes." Lissa's voice was cool. "You're a distant relation to August's family."

Elle raised her eyebrows and looked at August, who was frowning at Lissa.

"And now you and your daughter get to stay here for free." Lissa turned to August. "I'll see you soon."

"Yep," Elle said, "that's me and my daughter, the freeloaders."

"Excuse me?" Lissa turned to her, her mouth open and eyes wide.

Elle kept her voice calm. "I'm agreeing with what you said."

"Excuse me."

"Or course, I'll excuse you." Elle nodded. "It's obvious you don't realize how rude you are."

The blond man behind the reception desk turned a laugh into a cough, and the woman giggled, but Elle kept her gaze on the couple. August watched her, his face blank, not giving away any emotion. Lissa drew herself up an inch. With her four-inch heeled shoes, she was as tall as August.

It was a sad commentary on Elle's own self-image that she almost felt inferior.

Nah, she told herself. Not really.

"Do you know who I am?" Lissa's voice was icy.

"I said your name a few minutes ago. Have you forgotten already?"

"Elle," August said, his voice warning.

"Yes?"

"I think you'd better stop right there."

"You do, do you?" She gave him a lopsided smile, then there was a tug on her skirt, and she looked down. "Harper, honey?"

"Is that my Uncle August?"

"Yes, darling."

"You said he was nice." Her eyebrows shot down, her eyes accusing. "You said I'd like him."

"I did say that, didn't I?"

"He's not nice, Mommy." She shook her head, her expression solemn.

"I'm sorry, sweetie. He used to be nice, but people change."

Another giggle and a laugh came from the counter people.

"He was mean to you." Harper's voice was crabby, and she clearly wasn't ready to let go of the subject.

"I know, sweetie."

"I don't like him. I'm never going to like him."

A groan came from August. A sniff came from

his clinging companion. Another laugh and a giggle came from the counter.

"I'll get your suitcases." The man's voice was cheery, and Elle peered over her shoulder at the grinning blond guy stepping out from behind the counter.

"Thanks." She turned her back to August. "Chuck, right?"

"That's right. And you're Elle. Is this the princess?"

Harper giggled. Elle knelt and lifted her. "Yes, this is my princess," Elle said.

Harper's eyes closed, and she rested her head on Elle's shoulder. "I'm tired, Mommy."

"We've had a long ride. Let's go to our rooms, okay?"

"'Kay."

Elle nodded at Chuck, who was looking at her with his eyes hungry, as if she were a steak he wanted to feast on.

"I'm not sure where I'm staying," she said.

Chuck looked at August. "The empty chalet in the northwest corner? The one nearest yours?"

She didn't look at August, but she heard Lissa sniff, so she took that as a yes and headed out after Chuck, who was grinning again, clearly enjoying Lissa's annoyance. Elle held Harper, her arms crossed over Harper's back as Harper's head lay heavily on her shoulder. Just like that, already asleep. The deep sleep of innocence.

Chuck held the door open for her. As she headed onto the walkway, she heard muffled footsteps behind her, then the footsteps quickened next to her, and a long-fingered hand curved over her shoulder. Elle stopped and looked up, but she already knew who it was. The next instant, August stepped in front of her and bent to lift Harper out of her arms.

As he straightened, Harper's head flopped onto his shoulder. "I'll carry her." He started walking, not waiting for her consent. Just taking it for granted.

Elle took a deep breath and walked beside him. "Chuck, I can take the luggage," she said, looking behind her.

"No problem." He grinned and reached her side, the suitcases rolling on the walkway. "I can use the walk. If you lose anyone, it should be that mean guy on your other side."

She laughed as Chuck plowed ahead of them.

"The mean guy." August shook his head. "That's going to be all over town by tonight."

"Tonight?" She smirked. "More like by dinner."

"Thanks a lot for that."

"You're blaming *me*?"

"I am. You shouldn't have reacted as you did."

She raised her eyebrows. "You mean I shouldn't have replied in kind?"

He followed Chuck and her rolling suitcases. When they were halfway to the end of the resort, he said, "You're better than that."

"You're wrong. I'm better some days. Some days, I'm not." She kept her gaze straight ahead. "Today I'm tired and crabby. I've been driving for four hours with a four-year-old who never stopped talking, and I'm not perfect. Does your girlfriend have that excuse?"

He didn't reply, but ahead of them, Chuck

turned around. "Nope, but she thinks she's perfect."

Elle stopped and snapped around to August. He stopped, too, holding her daughter like she was someone precious, and it twisted her heart.

"I've been taking care of myself for a decade and my child for more than four years," she said. "I don't want any trouble with anyone. I don't start trouble. It's my first instinct to treat others with politeness and good-will. If someone doesn't reciprocate, I'm okay with it. Not everyone is a ray of sunshine. But if someone is mean to me, I'm a normal person, and I'm probably going to react in kind."

"What you don't see is that you're meaner."

"August, you have that all wrong." Her voice rose. She was tired of the subject, and these were the last words she was going to say on it. "I'm not *meaner* than her. I'm just *smarter*."

Ahead of them, Chuck cracked up into laughter. But she didn't look at Chuck, her eyes still on August as his face closed up, and he started walking.

Oh shit, she thought, catching up to his side. For a smart woman, she'd just done a very bad thing. She'd insulted his girlfriend.

It hurt her, because now she knew that he cared for Lissa. Until this second, she hadn't believed it. Ever since that day in the hospital, in her heart of hearts, she'd stupidly thought he'd always be hers.

He'd asked her to marry her, and she'd said no.

But she'd always had a sense that the offer would be open.

She'd been wrong. That door had shut when she hadn't been paying attention.

She'd been busy with the baby, the thrill of learning, interacting with her friends. Busy with her dissertation, music, life—everything but August. Never saying it aloud, but always thinking when she was ready for him, she could pick him up like a penny she'd dropped by accident and now she finally was ready to reach down, expecting that pretty copper coin to leap right into her palm.

Only to discover that she'd screwed up. He hadn't been waiting for her. Like her, he'd gone forward with his life. He'd found other interests. Other passions.

And another woman.

And now he would never be hers.

Twenty

Lissa was waiting for August in the cozy sitting area about twenty yards from the reception desk, with a fireplace on one side for winter guests and large windows on the other for a view of the dock and the bay. He headed over to her. Draped over a high-backed chair in the reception room as she checked out the messages on her phone, she could have been a "Modern Woman" portrait. When he stopped next to her, she raised her long neck and reached out to caress the side of his face.

"You're so amazingly handsome," she said.

He looked down at her face, at the flawless skin and the eyelashes that were like no one else's, long and dark and fanlike—and fake. She was like someone out of a reality TV show. Someone not quite real.

"Why did you do that?" he asked.

"Do what?" Her chin lifted.

He kept his gaze on her, not saying anything. A couple walked into the lobby. He heard their voices, talking about going on an artists' tour. If he hadn't been waiting for Lissa to answer, he would've asked the couple if they'd noticed the wood sculpture of a squirrel by the entranceway. The squirrel had a surprised, almost comical look on its face. One of August's favorite pieces. The sculptor lived only a couple miles away, and his studio was well worth looking at.

"You insulted my father's guest." He stayed by Lissa because this needed to be said. "Someone who's related to him."

"*She* insulted me. My father will—"

"You're telling your *father* on her?" His voice rose.

Laughter snorted from the desk. Lissa's complexion turned the color of a bad red wine. "Do you *have* to speak so loud?" she demanded in a low voice.

"I don't know what to say about you." He stepped back and crossed his arms over his chest as he wondered why he stood here, talking to her.

Their relationship had suited him. It had been convenient for him physically, and that's all he'd wanted. What they had together was basic. Nothing more than that.

She didn't expect anything from him except that he escort her to events. To dinner. To be a suitable partner at her side. So people would look at her and envy her. She was with the stepson of one of the wealthiest men in Trouble Bay. She was the daughter of the richest man. That's all he was to her.

He wasn't sure if she enjoyed sex with him, despite her loud moans, but he'd never questioned her about it. The truth was, he didn't care. They were using each other for their own means, and that had been all right with him.

Until Elle danced back into his life with her precocious daughter, who saw the darkness inside him.

He inhaled deeply, focusing his attention back to Lissa. If anything happened to her, he would feel sorry. But his world wouldn't end.

He wouldn't want to dive into the bay and never swim back up.

Lissa's eyelids lowered. "She did insult me. It wasn't my fault."

"She insulted you *back*. If you say something insulting to people, they get to insult you back."

"Usually they don't." She huffed out her breath. "I try to be polite, but it's not easy. People are annoying."

"Lissa, if you want people to help you, you need to treat them well."

"Darling, you are so wrong." She laughed lightly, getting to her feet, facing him, standing straight with her model body. "The more sarcastic you are, the more people admire you. That's been going on since..." She held out her hands and shrugged her thin shoulders, the movement balletic. "I don't know. Forever."

"Really? And that's working for you?"

"Yes." Her voice sharpened. "I know you believe people should be good, but—"

"What I believe," he said, "is that people should be kind. The woman you insulted today saved my life as a child."

Her breath sucked in. "I didn't mean—"

He shook his head, stopping her from lying. His heart felt heavy. If it had been Lissa driving down the street, she wouldn't have given his mother or him a second look. Not even if they'd been turning into snow people with icicles on their faces.

"My parents have a business here," he said, "and now it's my business, too. We are not better than our guests or our employees. We are not better than anyone who steps on our property. We don't treat anyone with meanness or cruelty."

"But she was—"

"Stop." He lowered his voice. "You were insulting to her, and she insulted you back."

"Well, if some people can't take it..." She hunched her shoulders.

He frowned. "You're not getting it."

"What?" Her voice was hard. "What am I not getting?"

He raised his eyes to hers. "She wasn't the one complaining. *You* are."

Her eyes flickered away from his.

"You should leave," he said.

"August." Her voice was low but intense. "You can't do this to me. You can't..." She glanced behind at the desk, then glared at what she saw there before dragging her gaze back to him. "You can't *drop me*. Don't do that, August."

He felt for her. Especially since he knew that Chuck had probably already told Melanie, the receptionist, that Elle had said she wasn't meaner than Lissa but she was smarter. Hell, by tonight, about three-quarters of the townspeople would know about it. They'd all be snickering at her. Snickering behind her back. Snickering to her face.

"Lissa, you need to understand. I cannot date a

woman who will offend my parents' guests or employees. Or a woman who thinks she's better than other town residents."

Her face was still frozen in either anger or disbelief that he was saying this to her. He backed away and started to turn. There didn't seem much else to—

"Don't." She grabbed the loose material of his shirt. "I'll be better. I'll change."

He stopped and looked at her. She was swallowing. He could see the hurt in her face, and it surprised him. He hadn't thought her emotions ran deep enough for her to feel hurt.

She let go, and a movement caught his eye. Her hand. It was shaking. A palsy-like movement. She saw the direction of his eyes and whipped her hand behind her back. "Please, August," she whispered. "Please."

He closed his eyes for a moment. When he opened them, she was staring at him, her chin up. As if daring him to drop her.

He couldn't do it. Not now.

And what did it matter? Nothing she'd done had changed anything.

He'd been using her. She'd been using him.

He'd only felt uncomfortable because Elle had called him out on it. Up to now, he'd liked the status quo. Up to now, Lissa's spiked tongue had even amused him. Something ugly inside of him had been drawn to that ugliness.

And because of it, he'd hurt Elle. He'd hurt her daughter. He'd hurt his mother, who couldn't understand why he was dating a woman like Lissa. And he'd hurt his father.

And now he'd hurt Lissa, too.

His problem wasn't her. His problem was himself. Ever since he'd gotten out of the service—

He stopped his thoughts, not wanting to go there. Not to that place he'd been avoiding since two years ago, when he'd become a civilian again.

"All right," he said. "Okay."

Her eyes closed, her only movement. But in that one small motion, he could see the relief on her face. Almost as if he'd saved her life the way Elle and her mother had saved him and his mother all those years ago.

Of course, it wasn't the same thing. But the desperation on her face was very real.

"Fine." She stood with a fluid movement, one hip thrust out, and her lips curved in a slight smile, as if she were posing for a photo. "Everything is all right now."

"For now." He kept his eyes on her. "I'll just repeat it once and never again. I can't date a woman who is rude to guests or residents."

"Darling." She lifted her hand and caressed the side of his face. "I'll be so sweet that people will gag when they see me. I know!" Her voice rose, her face animated. "My parents and I will have a huge party for Elle tomorrow night. We'll invite all the board members and all the families. She'll meet everyone who's important in Trouble Bay."

He opened his mouth to object—

"You said you thought she was going to look for a job now that she has her doctorate," Lissa continued. "Everyone in the area who matters will be there. This will be a good thing for her."

He closed his mouth. Perhaps it would be helpful for Elle. His parents were leaving most of the business to him now, though his mother still liked to check the rooms to make sure that everything was clean and tidy. Duke sometimes walked with her, but he preferred to check out structural and mechanical issues. Letting August know if anything needed to be replaced or fixed. But he left the business end to August.

Duke was a man's man. Though his family was one of the first families to settle in Trouble Bay, the people he cared for most were his wife and stepson. He certainly didn't give a rip who'd lived where two hundred years ago.

And his mother had never felt comfortable with Trouble Bay's founding families. She told him they were too "nose-in-the-air," which had made him laugh. But she had more in common with the workers. In the winter months, she was on a bowling team with the resort's housekeepers.

As he looked at Lissa, he realized that though she always smiled at his mother, she spoke to her slowly. As if Pilar might not understand her.

"I'll see you tomorrow," he said.

She stepped closer to him, put her arms around his shoulders, and kissed him.

He left his arms at his sides and didn't return the kiss, but she was smiling when she stepped back.

"Tomorrow," she said, then sashayed away, her hips swaying from side to side.

He watched her for a few seconds, then his gaze swept to the reception desk. Melanie was scowling. Chuck was watching Lissa's ass. He must have just returned from the chalet where Elle and Harper were staying. Easy to see what he was thinking right now.

Then August realized he would see Elle tonight.

The thought left a coldness in his chest.

Twenty-one

Elle felt restless, walking down a path to Uncle Duke and Aunt Pilar's home for dinner, Harper skipping at her side. The sun was shining but not as eye-hurting bright as earlier. The weather warm but not too hot.

She lifted her head and sniffed in the smells of sunshine, fresh air, trees, and the bay waters. It felt...magical. Like a place for lovers. And for the first time in a long time, she felt lover-less.

For the first time in a long time, she felt the yearning inside her for one.

She shivered. She knew why the yearning was there. Even if she didn't have a doctorate in psychology, it wouldn't have been hard to figure out.

August was seeing another woman.

"Mommy, are we going to see *that* man?"

Elle looked down at Harper's face that was twisted with sourness. "Sweetheart, August lives in the chalet by us. We'll see a lot of him. Try to be nice."

"He wasn't nice to you."

"I know, sweetie." She shrugged. He'd expected

more out of her. She'd expected more out of him.

She didn't know what had happened to him in the last four years, but he'd changed. He was...sadder. Seeing his sadness made her sad.

She squared her shoulders. *Everyone* changed. She should have expected change. And he'd been in the Marines. If anything had changed him, that was it.

And maybe he loved Lissa. The thought made her cringe inside, but she couldn't reject it just because she didn't want to believe it. He'd been with Lissa, who acted like she owned him. As if he belonged to her the way her designer shoes belonged to her.

Facts were facts.

"It's okay," she said. "Sometimes people are feeling bad, and when they're feeling bad, they aren't always nice. But we'll be nice to him."

"Not me. I don't have to be nice. I'm not a grown-up. I'm a *kid*."

Elle laughed down at her. "Kids have to be nice to people, too."

Harper's mouth set into a stubborn line, and Elle shook her head. She loved her daughter, but if Harper had one fault, it was that she could be stubborn.

"Uncle Duke and Aunt Pilar are August's mom and dad," Elle said. "If you're mean to him, we'll have to leave."

"Mommy, he needs to be nice to us."

Elle bent to hug her. "I'm glad you have an open mind."

Harper nodded but she frowned.

"What's wrong?" She kept walking, taking her

daughter's hand so Harper could skip alongside her.

"An open mind sounds icky."

"You're afraid your brains will fall out?" Elle asked.

Harper giggled, and a movement out of the corner of Elle's eye caught Elle's attention. She turned. *August.* She kept turning. *No Lissa.* "Hey."

He nodded. She could see on his face that he was as reluctant to see her as she'd been to see him. The realization brought her sadness. People changed, she reminded herself. Life changed. That's what was supposed to happen, and she needed to embrace it.

So she forced herself to smile and sound cheery to see him. He said hello without the fake smile and cheer, and it made her want to kick him. He could at least fake it. But women were much better at faking it than men. They had more experience.

The thought brought her a sad smile.

Her old friend was no longer a real friend, and she'd either have to accept it...or change it.

Twenty-two

"What do you want to do with your life?" Duke asked Elle.

Sitting on the chair in the patio, his legs out, August sipped his Door County wine, purposely keeping his body from stiffening and sitting up taller and looking at Elle. What she said shouldn't matter to him. When they were children, she'd changed his life for the better. But after his last tour, he'd decided that life was precious, and he had paid back enough.

It was time to live life for himself.

He was still starting to figure it out when she'd walked back into his life, with her red hair and her energy, her strong life force swirling out to everyone around her. Pulling them in like powerful magnets.

Only her life wasn't his life. She would leave again, and he didn't want to leave. Not anymore. This was his home.

Right now she watched her daughter petting his mom's small brown mutt with a happy pink tongue. Saying, "I love you, puppy. I love you." Obviously from the bliss on the dog's face, the love was reciprocated.

"I plan to be the best mom in the world." Elle grinned at Duke.

"You have a good start," he said. "How's that working financially?"

"So far no one is offering to pay me to be the world's best mom, but I have a plan."

"And what's that?" August asked. After the meal of barbecue ribs and corn, and his mother's *tres leches* strawberry cake, which she only made on special occasions, he didn't want to move off of the patio chair. If he was forced to, he might roll off.

Not his most attractive look, though it wasn't as if he had anyone around he wanted to impress.

Like hell, he told himself. *Like hell.*

"I'm not sure how it will work," she said. "I'd like to stay in the area. It's a good place to raise Harper." She made a face. "I have ideas, but in the meantime, I'm...um, co-writing a screenplay, actually, as crazy as it sounds. A friend and I are writing it together."

"A movie?" Pilar clapped her hands. She'd already cleared the dishes and taken them into their house, with Harper's and Elle's and his help, though she'd protested.

"I like helping," Harper had said, and Elle had bent to kiss her head.

He'd had to look away. He didn't know why it hurt, but it did.

The last overseas tour had changed him. He knew his actions since he came back—his unhappiness—hurt his mother and father. He needed to do something. But knowing he needed to change didn't make it happen.

"When we first met," he said now, "you read us a story about a fish and a cat and a dog."

Her face lit up, and she laughed. "I did?"

"Mommy, I'd like to know that story."

"I don't remember it." She put her hand on Harper's curly head. "We'll make up a story together, okay?"

Harper nodded vigorously.

"When is your friend coming?" August asked, changing the subject because it hurt. Like when he was a kid in Chicago, and he wanted so much he couldn't have.

"Next week," Elle said. "We rented a house in town."

"You shouldn't move into a house," Pilar said. "Stay here. Your friend can stay, too."

"Pilar's right," Duke said. "You're family."

Elle's eyes blinked fast, and her face softened, even as she shook her head. "I can't take advantage of you. This is your busiest time of year. I'm twenty-eight now. An adult. Staying a weekend is okay. Staying a month is *not* okay. I'm not going to freeload on you." As she said *freeload*, she shot a glance at August.

He narrowed his eyes back at her, and she grinned at him.

"Where will you be staying?" Pilar asked.

"Donna Grettle's house."

"Oh, no." Pilar frowned. "You can't stay there."

"Why? Is there a problem with the house?"

"I saw Donna this morning," Pilar said. "She said a *family* is staying at her place. A couple and a child."

There was silence for a minute, as if the breeze

121

slowed and the tree limbs stopped shaking like hula arms.

"Nate and I aren't a couple." Elle seemed to be purposely not looking at him. "He's my mother's age. In fact, they used to be close. We're sharing the house for a month while we write the screenplay. We chose it because it has three bedrooms, and two adults will make it easier to watch Harper."

A yelp came from the puppy, then Harper said, "I didn't mean to hurt you." Her voice had a cry in it as she looked at her mom, her eyebrows scrunched. "I love puppies, Mommy! Can we have one?"

Elle stood. In her casual green dress piped in blue, she looked closer to twenty than thirty. "I think it's bedtime for you. Nate will be bringing Misty with him. That will make you happy, right?"

"No. I want a puppy."

Elle laughed, and Pilar bent forward and told Harper that she could come over anytime and play with her puppy. Then Harper started crying. Big, heaving, overtired and overexcited sobs. Elle scooped Harper up, and Elle was so slight and Harper was wiggling, and it looked to August as if she'd drop to the ground in another two wiggles.

He stood and took one stride and pulled Harper to him, against his chest, her head slightly below his. "Time to go to bed, sweetheart."

She peered up at him, her cheeks cherry-red, tears shimmering in her eyes, and she reached up to put a pudgy little hand on each side of his cheek.

"I like you now," she said.

"That's good. I like you, too."

With a sigh of acceptance, she laid her head on his shoulder. The next second she was limp, her eyes closed, mouth open, exhaling and inhaling in sleep. Trusting him completely.

Elle thanked his parents again. August headed toward the chalet that was only a short walk from his. Two minutes, if they walked fast.

His parents' idea. Easy for him to see what they'd wanted.

Easy for all of them to see it wasn't going to happen.

So how odd was it that it felt so right carrying Harper on his shoulder?

And walking in silence next to Elle felt right, too. No words needed. Just an ache in his chest that grew stronger with every step.

At the chalet that Elle and Harper were staying in, Elle stood inside the entranceway and held out her arms for her daughter. He brushed past her, holding Harper.

"I'll carry her," he said, his voice low.

She followed him, and he felt her irritation. He walked through the sitting area, straight into the hallway. Except for the extra bedroom, it was like his chalet. Even the furniture was similar, comfortable yet stylish. His was in shades of gray with pops of blue and red. Hers was tan with pops of green and orange. Almost as if it were made for two redheads.

That thought made him curl up his lips as he turned into the smaller bedroom and put Harper down. She made a sleepy sound and turned onto her side as he straightened and stepped back. Just one step, as Elle took one step closer to him and he faced her but didn't move out of her way.

"The Normans are having a dinner party tomorrow night," he said. "You're invited. I already talked to my parents, and my mother wants to babysit."

"The Normans?" She made a face. "Lissa won't want me to be there."

"She invited you."

"You're kidding me."

"I don't kid."

"You used to."

"Never."

"That's...sad." She shivered, looking down, then up at him again. "Why would Lissa invite me? She doesn't like me."

"Out of the goodness of her heart."

One corner of her mouth lifted. "So you *do* kid."

He snorted a laugh, then stopped it. "It'd be good for you. All the important people in Trouble Bay will be there."

She gestured at her sleeping daughter, at him, then in the direction of his parents' house. "All the important people are here already."

He stared at her for what seemed a long moment before stepping back. "I'll pick you up at six-thirty tomorrow. Be ready."

Then he walked away quickly, while he still could.

Twenty-three

"The Norman home is ten thousand square feet and has six bathrooms." Pilar's eyes followed Harper as she hurried to the puppy, who was already rolling onto his back, ready to have his tummy rubbed.

"How many people live there?" Elle asked.

"Three," Duke said.

"What do three people need six bathrooms for?" Pilar put her hands on her hips. "That's two for each person. That's just wasteful."

"Maybe they pee a lot," Duke said.

She laughed and hit him in his shoulder. He grinned down at Pilar, about seven inches shorter than him.

Watching Duke and Pilar together made Elle feel good and that maybe love wasn't always hard. In her experience—from observation, education, and experience—what should have been one of the easiest things to do seemed to be the hardest.

She had her own theory. Maybe one day, she would write a paper. She could title it, "Why People Screw Themselves Up."

There was a reason so many people preferred

to live with dogs and cats instead of other humans. Animals were easier to live with than people. And usually *much* easier to love. Humans made everything complicated.

"We should go," August said.

She nodded. August had said that Lissa was doing this for her, but she suspected that if she were crossing a street and a car was racing straight toward her, and Lissa was on the other side of the street, the only person to witness the runaway car, Lissa would press her lips together and say nothing and do nothing.

Or perhaps she might be the driver of the car. As she sped away, she would be chortling happily.

Elle called good-bye to Harper, who looked up from the puppy, her face gloriously glowing.

Seeing Harper happy made Elle smile. She thanked Pilar for watching Harper tonight, and Pilar said, "No, we thank you."

"If we're babysitting," Duke says, "it gives us an excuse not to go to the Normans' place."

She raised her eyebrows, but Duke just shook his head, and Pilar was already heading over to Harper and the puppy. Over her shoulder, Pilar said, "August, when am I going to get one of these?"

He grabbed Elle's arms and tugged her toward the door. "Mom, if you want another puppy, I'll take you to the Humane Society tomorrow."

"Oh, you—"

"Bye, sweetheart," Elle said again. Harper called out good-bye but this time didn't look up from the puppy. Elle sighed. Impossible to compete against a puppy.

In another ten years, Harper's distraction might be a boy, but Elle didn't like to think about it.

August was silent as they drove down the curving road to the Normans' bayside home. She had a thousand questions but started with one.

"Why is your girlfriend doing this?"

"You asked me yesterday."

"So I did. And you told me out of the goodness of her heart. Really, August? Do I have *gullible* tattooed on my forehead?"

There was silence as he slowed and turned onto the driveway. The sky was light blue with fluffy white clouds, but the brightness of the day was fading, the sun edging downward.

"I wouldn't call her my girlfriend. We've been seeing each other, that's all."

"Ah," she said. She knew what *seeing each other* meant.

"*Dating.*" He slanted a dark look, as if he could see into her mind. "It's been convenient. Nothing more than that."

She made a face but didn't say anything. This man she was sitting next to was not the same man she'd last known four years ago.

They neared the lake house that was bigger than some schools Elle had seen. She sat up, taking in the home that was made for real estate clichés. *Sprawling. Pristine. Panoramic views.*

Her mother was going to be surprised. Elle was pretty sure that when they'd lived in the area, the Normans' home had just been a big two-story.

"Lissa's parents must be doing well," she said.

"John Norman's a property developer." August

parked the car behind a Jeep that had seen a few miles. There were more than a dozen cars altogether, from old clunkers to shiny, new SUVs and sports cars. "The biggest in the area. He's spread out over Door County now."

"Isn't he the chairman of the town board, too?" she asked. "Isn't that a conflict of interest?"

"Are you here to make friends?" he asked. "Or are you here to make enemies?"

"I'm here to write a screenplay."

"And scout around for a job." He opened his car door and stepped out.

She hopped out of the passenger side. He was waiting for her at the front of the car, and he turned and started walking, with her at his side.

"My mother has a big mouth," she said.

"It made my parents happy."

"I'm not asking your parents. What about you?"

He didn't reply for a moment, and their steps slowed. "You changed my life once." His resonating voice lowered. "I think you might change it again."

"Sometimes we need a change."

He stopped. "But what if we don't?"

"Don't you?"

He stepped forward, not answering. She put her hand on his arm. He froze.

"Do you *want* me to stay?"

"My parents do." He didn't look at her.

"I'm not asking your parents. What about you? If you say no, I'll go."

A moment went by, and she felt frozen in time. A cool breeze blew through the trees, and goose bumps rose on her arms. He looked at her. "It's not my choice, it's yours."

Then he was walking again, and so was she, having to hurry to keep up with his long strides. But inside her, she was celebrating. If he didn't want her to be here, he would have said *no.*

So if that wasn't a *no*, then it must be a *yes.*

She wanted to laugh and tell him, *I know what you mean.* But he was a man, and they had that stubborn gene inside them.

Yes, she knew that not all men were the same, and not all men were stubborn. Just all the ones she'd known.

Instead, she laughed, feeling...happy as she headed to the front door. Dancing-in-the-rain, walking-on-air happy.

The double front doors with too much brass opened, and, framed by the doorway, Lissa stood with her short, sassy dark hair, high cheekbones, and doe-like brown eyes. She wore a dress that was purple and black, perfect for the weather, perfect for her hair and makeup and coloring. Sliding down her thin body that wasn't thin in the places men cared about—booty and boobs, the two Bs. And she was tall and held herself like a queen.

But yesterday, she'd been bitchy, and some of the happiest people that Elle knew were happy because they lived life fully, not because they looked perfect in a mirror, and that was the person Elle strived to be.

So she stretched a smile on her face and reminded herself that Lissa was doing this for her and that she was going to enjoy herself no matter what.

Squaring her shoulders, she marched forward, like a soldier going into battle.

Twenty-four

The party was more fun than Elle had expected. She was talking to a cousin of Sylvia's, Sheldon Blakeslee, and Adrian, his partner at his hat shop and in his life, when John Norman interrupted their conversation. She turned to him reluctantly.

"What made you decide to be a psychologist?" John Norman asked, though as it came out of his mouth, it sounded more like a command.

His wife, Janet Norman, leaned forward, and Elle had to hold her ground, ignoring an instinct to step back. Lissa's parents were tall like their daughter. Though they were nowhere as thin, they weren't too heavy, either. Instead, they were sleek and oiled. No bulges, as if under their clothes, they were tightly bound in a clingy plastic wrap.

"I find people interesting," Elle said.

"Your mother was like that." Janet's voice was disapproving. If her forehead had been able to move, it would have been creased.

"My mother's still like that."

"Where is she now?"

"Rome."

"What's she doing in Rome?" John asked.

"I'm pretty sure she's enjoying herself with her new lover."

Their mouths dropped open, and a titter came from Sylvia, who'd joined their small group. She looked like Grace Kelly in her Princess of Monaco stage of life, only thinner. Not the person Elle would have expected to appreciate her mother's activities, but that was one of the things Elle enjoyed about people. Their surprises, good and bad.

"Studying people is the coolest job ever." Elle grinned at Sylvia before turning back to John and Janet.

"Are you looking for a job in one of our school systems?" Janet Norman's face was pinched. "We are more conservative here."

Elle stopped herself from looking at their daughter, who was draped over the side of August like she was his accessory, her breasts pressed into his arm.

"I'm co-writing a screenplay," she said.

"Oh? You expect to sell it?" Janet's voice was cool.

"I only expect to co-write it." Keeping her smile on, like a form of war paint, she turned to Sylvia. When she and August had first walked into the Normans' house, Lissa had leeched onto August's arm, then proceeded to introduce her to the thirty or so guests, aged from the seventies to the low thirties. Almost all of them had a place on the town board or were related to someone on the board.

"Usually, it's the expectation to sell the script," John said, demanding her attention.

"That would be nice." She smiled, tight-lipped. She wasn't going to tell him that four of Nate's screenplays had been made into movies. That had been over thirty years of writing, which made it sound less impressive.

She turned back to Sylvia. "It's so nice to meet you again. I know it's been a long time, but I remember you from Duke's wedding."

Sylvia's eyebrows shot up and her mouth opened, but no words came out. On her face, Elle could see not just surprise but shock, too.

"You were beautiful," Elle went on. "And you smiled so nicely at me. When my mom and I moved to Madison, we saw *Cinderella* at the theater, and I can remember insisting to her that Chuck's mom was the real fairy godmother. I never forgot you."

"Well!" Janet's tone was hearty. "That's quite a compliment, Sylvia."

"You're *still* beautiful," Elle said, as tears moistened Sylvia's eyes. "You still look like a fairy godmother."

"Sylvia's beautiful inside and out." A shorter woman in baggy knit pants and a silken T-shirt put her hand on Sylvia's arm. Elle couldn't remember her name, but she did something at the community hall with fish fries. "When I broke my arm, Sylvia came to my restaurant and helped make the batter. Not just once. For two weeks! Every day! And she made her son help, too. She's an angel."

Sylvia's face flamed. "Kathy, you helped me when I needed help, too."

"Of course I did. That's what friends are for."

"It's probably written in Sylvia's book of rules," Janet Norman said. "'Help thy neighbors in need.'" She smiled smugly. "I went to school with Sylvia, and she used to have a list of rules on how to act. She's the planning commission chairperson, and John said she makes sure they observe all the rules."

As she stopped talking, there was a moment of dead silence, one of the lulls of conversation that Elle noticed happened in parties at the most embarrassing times. Everyone seemed to be staring in horror at Sylvia and Janet except for John Norman, who was nodding and smiling, and Lissa, who was staring at the ceiling as if she wanted to be someplace else. Janet was still smiling, but Sylvia had a look of horror on her face.

Elle instinctively moved to Sylvia's side. As she did, August said, "The town board is lucky to have someone who is aware of the rules. You wouldn't want to get sued."

"You're right there," another man said. "I'm glad Sylvia's on the board."

"And me," said another woman, a chubbier woman with graying hair who looked vaguely familiar to Elle. She pushed between Elle and Sylvia, putting her hand on Sylvia's left arm, so she and the other woman were standing like sentries on either side of her. "Sylvia is a godsend and a credit to the community."

The smugness on Janet's face slowly vanished, and she looked confused, clearly unsure what had happened. One of those people so self-obsessed that she didn't get it. Like a cat who'd plopped down on the dog's bed and wouldn't move off of it.

Elle looked away from her. In a cat, it was cute. In a person, it was ugly.

People started talking, and the two ladies on either side of Sylvia took her off to the other end of the room, away from Janet Norman. In their place, two women in their early thirties stopped in front of Elle and told her about the jewelry shop they owned together.

Elle tried to give them her attention, but just a few feet away, she saw Lissa talking animatedly to August, whose expression was grave. Stone-like. Staring at nothing.

She swallowed and forced herself to pay attention to the two women instead of the burning question in her mind.

What happened to August? What happened?

Twenty-five

Sitting in her room in back of the kitchen with moonlight shimmering into the back window, Sylvia sobbed. Quietly. No one was likely to hear her, but there was a couple in the Amelia and John Suite above her, and she couldn't let them hear their hostess crying.

She'd never been so humiliated in her life. Not when Charley had been catting around town, and she'd been aware that everyone knew.

Not even after the storm that had destroyed the roof and upper story of her house and the insurance agent had cheated her.

She'd been too furious to feel humiliation. In her anger, there had been no room for embarrassment.

But tonight... What that bitch Janet had said...

How *dare* she? How dare that bitch? That awful, terrible, unmannerly bitch who everyone in town knew had had a facelift and a boob lift and probably a butt lift, too.

When it was obvious that what she truly needed was a character lift.

But after those first horrible moments that had

seemed to last forever...everything had changed for Sylvia. It had felt as if a sandwich of love surrounded her. Her two friends on either side. And not just them, but almost everyone in the room had been looking at her with respect and admiration and all the emotions that people normally didn't express until the person was dying—and often not then. Usually people said those words of praise only at funerals.

But she was alive, and now she knew that she had her friends' respect and affection.

All these years she'd wondered. She was not an emotional person. Some people were. People like Brenda Forsythe, who'd been teaching first grade at the elementary school for over twenty years. She cried during graduations. She cried on the first day of school. She cried when people got married. She cried when people got divorced. For heaven's sake, she'd even cried once when Sylvia told her she'd had a root canal.

All that emotion made Sylvia weary, and she avoided Brenda, who she secretly thought of as the Watering Pot.

Yet, here she was, going through a box of tissues, and doing a pretty damn good Brenda imitation.

She felt like the actress who'd won the Oscar the second time and in her acceptance speech said, "You like me!"

And even before her friends had come to her support, Elle Styles had said all those wonderful things.

Telling her she was like the fairy godmother in Cinderella...

If any young woman had said that, she would have been pleased. But this had been from *That Girl*—that redheaded girl from Duke's wedding who had changed her life all those years ago when she'd been walking down a path of bitterness. The small child had radiated joy at a time that should have been like poison to Sylvia's soul. Instead, the purity of the child's happiness had been a revelation. The catalyst to pull the poison out of Sylvia's heart.

All these years later, she could still recall the awe she'd felt. It was as if she'd seen the parting of the seas or some other Biblical miracle. It had changed her from the inside out.

If not for that one-hundred-eighty-degree change of heart, her friends would not have defended her tonight.

If not for that one night, that one joyful face, so many other things might have been different. She might have clung to her bitterness—in fact, she was sure she would have clung on to it like John Norman clung to his comb-over, even though everyone snickered at him and it made him look like an idiot.

And if she'd hung on to her bitterness against Charley, it would have embittered Chuck, who resembled his father with his golden looks and his easy personality. And she had to face it, like his father, Chuck was no ball of fire.

But Chuck wasn't a cheater. He wasn't a drunk or a druggie. And he wasn't a gambler. At his heart, he was a good man. Yet she could see that he liked the easy way. Perhaps because of his father's example, she'd always watched him.

Always expected him to screw up.

When she'd stopped finding faults, he'd changed. It wasn't that love had changed him—she'd always loved him—it was her acceptance. Her belief that he would be better. And because of that, she had a son who, though he wasn't perfect, was a man she thought would be a good man.

All this because of that one night, Duke's wedding to another woman, that at first she'd thought was going to be one of the worst nights in her life.

And, yes, she was not perfect. She had regressed, and she was not sorry for the incident with the insurance agent. Not sorry at all.

If the same circumstances were in place, she would do it again.

It was okay to stumble. She gave herself the same acceptance and compassion that she gave others. Killing was part of her nature. She accepted that. But only when the other person was so bad that he or she deserved it.

And though she knew it was considered to be morally wrong—not to mention criminally—she couldn't say she was sorry.

After all, everyone had faults.

But oh, but oh, but oh...

People loved her. *Loved her.*

People cared. *Cared.*

For her.

And all these years, the small redheaded girl with the radiant smile had thought of her as a fairy godmother.

She grabbed a tissue from the box at the side of her bed, and she blew into it noisily.

Her life might not have been perfect, but at this second, only one thought marred her happiness. The thought that Elle's mother was careless and selfish, in Rome with a male friend instead of watching over her daughter and granddaughter.

Someone should be taking care of Elle and her daughter. Yes, Elle was an adult, and she seemed intelligent and responsible. Even though her child had been born out of wedlock. Nowadays, that was nothing. In fact, she wished she'd had Chuck without marrying Charley. She would've been better off.

And Charley might still be alive.

But she didn't want to think about that. Though Charley had deserved what had happened to him, he was her son's father. And she certainly didn't believe in gloating.

She switched her thoughts back to Elle. *Focus. Focus.* Probably no one was going to harm her here in Door County. But one never knew, and it didn't hurt to keep an eye on her.

Twenty-six

"Here we are." August parked in the parking lot of the resort. "I'll walk you to my parents' place."

Elle curved her hand over his right arm. "We should talk."

He froze for a second before turning to her. "Do you know what the worst three words a man can hear are?"

She released his arm. "I have a gun?"

"That's four words."

"This is the IRS."

"Another four words."

"I'm pregnant."

"Two words. How did you get through college if you can't count to three?"

"I must have missed the 'count to three' math test." She made a face. She hadn't skipped the 'I'm pregnant' test. She'd passed that one with flying colors.

"More like you ignored it," he said, clearly still stuck on the three words. "You're not letting me go, are you?"

"You're almost a foot taller than I am. If you

really want to get away from me, you could shake me off, open the door, and walk away."

"My mother would be embarrassed."

She laughed softly. It was dark out except for the moonlight and the few lights in the parking lot that made his face almost colorless. But he would never be black and white to her. He was the boy she'd begged her mother to pick up all those years ago. And if she saw him on the side of the road now, his car broken, she'd do the same thing. And so would a lot of other women. Just looking at him made her ache. Made her want more of him. Probably because they were so close, she could hear his exhale and see the stiffness ease out of his body.

In turn, her own body relaxed.

"I didn't know your mother embarrassed so easily," she said, "but I certainly wouldn't want you to be rude. For your mother's sake, of course."

"Are you flirting with me?" His voice was low.

In her chest, her heart thumped. "Would you like it if I were flirting with you?"

"That's a psychologist question."

"Is it? Or is it a question of a woman who thinks you're handsome and sexy?"

His left eyebrow quirked. "This from a woman who turned down my proposal of marriage."

"You mean a woman who'd just had a baby ripped out of her vagina?" She put her hand on his arm again, and he tensed.

"It was because of the baby that I asked you to marry me."

She pulled her hand away from him a second

time. She closed her eyes. Only for a few seconds. Then she opened them and exhaled.

"That's right. You were worried about giving my baby a father." She reached for the door handle and opened the door. "Good night, August."

She got out of the car and closed the door. Only as she walked across the grass to his parents' house did she realize she hoped he would call her name. Ask her to come back to him.

Or to not even say anything. If he just strode up to her to walk her and Harper back to their chalet. That would be more his style.

But he did neither.

Twenty-seven

Sitting on the gray carpet in the living room of Donna Grettle's house while Donna visited her sister in Nashville, Harper pouted at a picture book with images of a black and green caterpillar. "Mommy, I miss the puppy. I miss Grandma Pilar. I miss Grandpa Duke. I miss Uncle August."

Elle pushed back her hair behind her ears. After putting away all their clothes, she felt sweaty. The three-bedroom bungalow on the block behind Sylvia's much nicer bed-and-breakfast had air conditioning, but she didn't know how to turn it on.

She felt like an idiot, but she'd never been good at things like that. She'd wait for Nate to get here, or she'd walk across the alley to Sylvia's house. Sylvia or Chuck would tell her how to turn on the air conditioning.

One person she wasn't going to ask was August. She didn't need him. He was too difficult. Difficult people were interesting in her professional life, but they were trouble in her personal life.

She was drawn to him like metal fragments

were drawn to giant-sized magnets, but unlike metal fragments, she had a brain and could step back from his DNA that was calling *come here, baby* to her DNA.

"You know what I miss?" she asked Harper, shutting off her thoughts of August.

"What?"

She took a step toward Harper, wiggling her fingers. "I miss my tickle bunny."

Harper screamed, hopped up to her feet, and ran, giggling wildly.

Elle chased after her. She let her get away in the kitchen and circle back to the living room, where she caught Harper and tickled her while she screamed with laughter. Elle laughed, too, until finally Elle pulled back to let them both catch their breath.

The screen door clanged. "Hey!" a man's voice called. "No fair having too much fun without me."

They were both sprawled on the carpet, and Elle had to use her hands to push up, her stomach hurting from laughing so hard. Harper jumped up right away, not needing any help.

"Uncle Nate!" she screamed. "You're here."

"Of course I'm here." The screen door closed behind the gray-haired man wearing baggy shorts and a black Rolling Stones T-shirt who stood just inside the front door. He bent to set down a pet carrier. "You doubted me?"

"No!" She ran up to him, and he bent to hug her. A meow came from the carrier, and Harper pushed away from him and called out, "Misty!"

She dropped to her knees and took out the big gray-and-white cat who meowed loudly, clearly complaining about the indignities she'd endured since Harper and Elle had left Madison.

Now it was Elle's turn to hug Nate. They stepped apart, and she grinned at the man who she'd once hoped would be her stepfather, but instead he'd become a good friend to her mother and her. He grinned back at her, smile lines crinkling.

"You smell like the city," she said.

"Gotta say, Elle, you smell a little sweaty."

She wrinkled her nose. "I can't figure out how to turn on the air conditioner."

His laughter boomed, and the sound made her grin. She pushed up on her toes and hugged him again. "I missed you so much."

"Missed you, too, doll."

A noise came from the screen door.

"I wish my mom had married you." Still grinning, she stepped back and around him, then blinked at August staring at her through the screen door, his expression...like someone who was about to throw up.

"Hey," she said, "did I forget something?"

He shook his head. "My mom just wanted to know if everything is well."

"Your mom's sweet, but we're fine, aren't we, Harper?"

"Did you bring Puppy with you?"

"Sorry. No puppy."

Her lower lip puffed out. "I miss Puppy."

"I'm sure Puppy misses you, too. But you can come visit."

"You have Misty," Elle said and shook her head. "But no puppy. Poor, deprived child."

Harper nodded vigorously. "I'm 'prived."

Both men laughed.

Shaking her head, Elle pushed open the screen door. "Come in and meet my writing partner in crime. August Reyes, meet Nate Finkelstein."

"Your screenplay is about crime?" He stepped in and shook hands with Nate, standing a head taller and straighter and twenty-some years younger than the older man who wore black-rimmed glasses and had bushy eyebrows and an impressively sized nose. Nate liked to say it had to be big to match his big brains.

"It's about politics," Nate said.

"And a love story," Elle said.

August cocked an eyebrow. "Which part is the crime?"

Nate chuckled. "Take your choice. As long as you're here, how are you at turning on air conditioners? And what kind of restaurants are around here?"

August stepped farther into the house. "I'll get the air. As for restaurants, there aren't any bad places."

"Spoken like a good Chamber of Commerce member." Nate opened the front screen door.

"You find a bad meal, the next one's on me."

"I can see this is a friendly town. Right now I need to bring in my suitcase and unpack."

The screen door closed behind him, and Elle followed August to the hallway. He stopped in front of the thermostat that she'd somehow walked by about a dozen times already but hadn't noticed.

"What's with you?" she demanded.

August didn't look at her as he reached up to adjust the thermostat.

"You're giving off mixed signals." She crossed her arms. "I don't like them."

The air conditioner turned on with a small roar.

"I want to kick you," she said.

"That's funny." August turned to her, his eyes burning into hers so deep she could feel the heat. "I want to kiss you."

She stared at him. He stared at her. And then the front screen door opened, and Nate grunted, and something banged down onto the living room carpet.

"Go ahead," she said, her voice low and raw, her gaze not leaving August's eyes. "Do it."

He stepped back. "I don't like audiences."

"Chicken."

He turned away, stepping into the living room, saying something to Nate, who replied with a laugh in his voice, and then calling good-bye to Harper, who said good-bye to him from her and from Misty the cat.

And all this time she stood in the hallway, her fists closed tightly, breathing hard, still wanting to kick him.

Twenty-eight

"I've seen Elle's screenwriter partner," Angela Dufort whispered in the supermarket aisle over strawberries, her bulldog-like jowls wiggling. "He's Jewish."

Sylvia sighed in disappointment at the pale strawberries. In another week, the Stewarts' farm would be selling them. Until then, they would have to make do with the imported strawberries.

"Good for her," she said. "In that case, I hope he's funny as well as smart."

Angela sniffed. "He's older than she is, and they're probably not sleeping together."

Sylvia stepped to the onion bins, stopping at the sweet onions. She loved sweet onions. In fact, she loved most vegetables and fruits. What she hated was gossip, though, of course, she indulged. After all, she was human.

"It's a business association. I never imagined it would be anything else."

"I bet Lissa Norman and her parents hoped it was something else," Angela said.

Sylvia put her hand over her mouth to stifle a

laugh. Looking up, she saw Angela smirking at her. They both snickered.

Angela leaned over the sweet potatoes and glanced around. A move that Sylvia approved of. John and Janet Norman were like ticks. You never knew you'd been bitten by one until you'd spent a few thousand dollars on medical tests and listened to the doleful pronouncement of the doctor who should've looked for the little suckers first thing instead of last. With John and Janet Norman, it was the same thing.

Sylvia's grandfather had a saying about the Normans. *If you drop a penny and the Normans are around, better jump out of the way as quick as you can or you'll get trampled by the stampede.*

"The Normans are pretty confident about Lissa's chances with August," Angela said. "The odds are going up that he'll marry her."

Sylvia shrugged. She couldn't always tell when a man was in love, but she could tell when a man wasn't. August certainly was not.

Some people were going to lose money.

And others—mainly herself—were going to win big.

"I'll take those odds," she said.

Angela looked at her sharply. Behind her, Sylvia could see a man bending over the lemons in a black T-shirt and khakis that came to his knees, exposing his muscular calves below. He seemed to be thoroughly inspecting the fruit. A man who took his lemons seriously.

"Did you bet on Lissa Norman?" Angela whispered.

Sylvia snapped her attention back to Angela. "I

really shouldn't say anything."

"You don't think he'll marry her, do you?"

Sylvia looked down. "Angela, whether he'll marry Lissa or not is none of my business."

"I won't tell anyone." Angela held up her right hand, as if they were in court. "But you know that my siding is over thirty years old. I really need new siding."

Sylvia winced for Angela. Though she thought Angela was silly, they had known each other for many years. Besides, Sylvia knew what it was like to be a single woman trying to get by on not a lot of money. "I'm not the best barometer of lovers," she said slowly, "but August is not in love with her."

"If he's in lust with her," Angela scowled, "that's all most men need to marry a woman."

"That wasn't true even when we were young." Sylvia heaved a breath. "And it's certainly not necessary for men to marry for sex. Or for women, either. Besides, Chuck thinks August is about to dump her." She lowered her voice. "I hope you won't tell anyone I said that."

"I won't." Angela made a sign of the cross over her heavy, pendulous breasts. "Thank you, Sylvia, thank you. I have to go and make a financial transaction. That's for the tip on the...um, strawberries." She winked, then rushed out of the fruit aisle.

Sylvia winced, watching her go. She hoped she was right. She'd like to see Angela with new siding.

A clearing throat made her snap around.

The man who'd been inspecting the lemons stood in front of Sylvia, and she hadn't noticed that he'd moved. The surprise made her gape at him, as if she were staring at a movie star, though there was nothing movie-star-ish about his face. Instead, there was humor in his face. A brightness. He wore glasses. His nose was...well, he would never have to worry about his glasses sliding off his nose. His eyes were brown and lively as he inspected her face.

"You're Elle's partner." Her voice was sharp, her complexion warm. He must have overheard her and Angela talk about him. Instead of moving away, like most people, he'd stuck around and pretended to be interested in the produce.

She was determined to ignore her embarrassment. Of course Angela and she had talked about him. He was a stranger. It was the way of all people to talk about new people in town. How else would they know who was safe or not? Gossip had always been that way, and it would always be that way.

"I'm Nate," he said. "Nate Finkelstein."

She raised her eyebrows. "An interesting last name."

"I have the nose." He tapped the end of what her father would have called a 'schnoz.' "I may as well have the name. There's no hiding who I am."

"I can see that. And why should you?"

"That's what I've always thought. And without even knowing me personally, a very wise woman realized that just by my name, I'm funny and smart."

Her blood felt like it was flowing faster. The neurons in her brain were speeding up. This man was...interesting. He would keep a person on her toes. Certainly when he was around, a person would not be bored.

"I can tell that you live up to your name," she said.

"You know mine, but I don't have the pleasure of yours."

"Sylvia Pascal. I'm a friend of Elle's."

"Lucky Elle."

She felt her skin warm again. This man didn't look like a movie star. In fact, he was on the short side, and some people might say he was unattractive. But he had the charm and confidence of a movie star. A star with character, which to her was more important than good looks. After all, she'd been married to a handsome man without character, and that hadn't ended well for either of them.

Really, young women should be warned against good-looking young men. If only she could stand in front of an auditorium of high school girls—or even middle school—to warn them.

That could never be. The truth might set some people free, but it would send her to jail.

But this man was looking at her with a twinkle in his eyes, and she was feeling warm in a way that she hadn't felt in many years. In a way she hadn't allowed herself to feel. Not after the marriage that she normally tried not to think about. She'd been badly treated, and it had made her angry. She'd been hurt.

Some people might say her heart had been broken.

Other people, the ones who'd known her back then, would have said she'd had such a rigid personality that when something went wrong, she couldn't see past her rules.

"Are you all right?" he asked, his voice seeming to come from far away.

She shook her head. Inside her chest, her heart was pounding. "I'm thinking of my past sins."

"Everyone has past sins. Does thinking about them make you unhappy?"

"This is a very odd conversation." She glanced around. Still no one else in the produce aisle, as if they were in a small pocket of quiet.

He shrugged. "Then stop thinking about old sins."

"Just like that?"

"Perhaps not just like that. Dancing helps. Do you like to dance?"

She nodded. It had been a long time since she'd danced. She couldn't remember the last time.

"I'm settling in tonight," he continued, "but would you like to go for a dinner and a dance soon?"

"I don't know. Are you married?"

"No, but that's a good question. Any others?"

She thought about it, then shook her head. Nothing he'd done in his life could be as bad as anything she'd done in her life. At least, by normal standards. And if he'd done what she'd done, he wouldn't tell her anymore than she would tell him.

"Then expect to hear from me soon," he said.

"It's been a long time since I've gone to dinner with a man."

"You're beautiful. Are the men around here all blind?"

She smiled slightly and bowed her head. Perhaps at one time in her life, she'd taken pride in her even features and her body that wasn't too thin or too curvy, too tall or too short. And then there was her blond hair that waved but didn't frizz. Even her intelligence was a matter of pride.

As if she had everything. But now she knew that, despite all her physical and mental attributes, she was no better than anyone else. She'd had to find that out the hard way.

"It's been my decision not to date. My choice."

"What a waste."

She raised her eyes and held his gaze. Not a waste. She'd already killed two men. They'd both deserved it, but that didn't mean she had to be the one to end their lying, cheating lives. If it were fair game to kill people who deserved death, there might not be many live people left in the world.

"We can make up for lost time." Nate smiled. "I'll see you soon, Sylvia Pascal." He nodded, then walked away from her, his step jaunty. A man who, even from the back, gave the impression of being satisfied with himself.

As she watched him, something stirred inside her.

Excitement. Sexual excitement.

She put her hands over her cheeks, and her cheeks were warm again. Whatever happened, she told herself, this time would be different. This time, she didn't plan to kill the man she wanted to sleep with.

Twenty-nine

The phone's ring snapped Elle into wakefulness. Her room was pitch black, and she fumbled for the phone on the small table next to her bed. Her mind was fuzzy with sleep, though her heart was beating too fast. It must be her mom in Rome, and Rome time was seven hours ahead of Wisconsin time. Her mother was impetuous, but she wasn't inconsiderate. For her to wake up Elle in the middle of the night, it must be important.

But as she glanced at the eerie, green-lit phone number display, she saw it was local.

Who would...?

She clicked on the phone, sitting in the darkness. "Hello," she said. "Who is this?"

"Help me. Help me." The voice was deep, but the words were broken.

"August? Is that you?" Her heartbeat hammered.

"Help me."

"Where are you? Are you home?"

There was silence.

"August." She threw off her cover, jerked out of

the middle of a REM sleep cycle, her heartbeat accelerated. "Are you home? Answer me."

She could hear breathing on the phone, and she closed her eyes for a second. Good. He was still there.

Still alive.

What horrible thing had happened to him?

"Do you want me to call your mom?"

"No. Just...want help."

"I'll help you." She was shaking. "Where are you? Should I call the ambulance? The sheriff?" There was more silence. "Answer me, August! Answer me."

"Just you, Elle. Just you."

She stood, her eyes adjusted enough to see the boxy shape of the dresser. She stepped around it, her hand out to feel for the light switch on the wall between the dresser and the door.

"Are you drunk?" she asked. "Sick?"

The sound he made could have been a laugh or a cry.

She found the light switch and pushed it up, blinking at the sudden brightness. "Tell me now, or I'll call the sheriff." Before he could answer, she added, "And your mom."

"Home," he said, her threat to call his mother working. "I'm home. Help. Me."

"I'll be there as soon as I can. Don't do anything... August?" The phone had a dead sound. He didn't answer. "August," she repeated, the high pitch of her voice even louder than the wild beating of her heart.

No answer. Crap. She turned the phone off and set it down, then traded her sleep camisole top and loose purple bottoms for a pair of cotton slacks and a T-shirt, not bothering with a bra. The swap took less than a minute, the camisole and bottoms left on the floor. She grabbed her phone again and opened the door, and there in the hallway was her sleepy-looking writing partner, rubbing his right eye beneath his glasses.

"That your mom?" he asked.

A meow, the sound a question mark, brought her attention to Misty near his feet, looking up at Elle with her head tilted, as if she wanted to hear her answer, too.

She shook her head at the cat and then Nate. "A friend needs me. Harper isn't likely to wake up, but if she does, will you take care of her?"

"Of course. You want to talk about it?"

"I've got to go. If Harper needs me, call me."

He half smiled. "It's a man, isn't it?"

She stepped past him. "It's a *friend*."

He laughed low in his throat. "I know that look on your face. It's a man."

She kept walking. Yes, August was a man, but he was a friend first, and that's why she was hurrying to help him. She wasn't going to let a friend down, no matter what his sex.

Thirty

August was sick at heart. That's all he knew. Sick in spirit. And just in case he was sick physically, he had a pail on the carpet next to his couch.

The doorbell rang, but he didn't answer. The bell rang again, and this time August groaned.

The door opened, someone coming in.

He turned his head, and it felt like a dream, Elle rushing into the room, her thick red hair kinked into spirals and bouncing off of her shoulders. If his eyes weren't playing tricks on him, her perfectly sized breasts were bouncing nicely, too. She definitely wasn't wearing a bra.

Even though he'd drunk too much today, he would have to be blacked out not to notice her breasts. He liked women's breasts. He liked pretty much all parts of their bodies, and he'd spent time wondering what Elle's would look like naked. Spent too much time wondering about it.

But not now. This wasn't a good time. In fact, it was a bad time. A very bad time.

"Go 'way," he muttered.

She closed the door behind her, and he wasn't

surprised that she'd ignored him. "You called me. You asked for help."

"No, I didn't."

"Aw, August." She got down on her knees next to the bucket, and she ran her fingers through his hair that he knew must be hot and sweaty. It felt good, and he craned his head toward her. Like a dog, he thought in his muddled mind. A dog that wanted to be petted.

He mumbled something.

"What?" she asked, her voice soft. Soothing.

"Feels good," he said.

"That's nice." She continued to stroke his head. "You want to tell me what your problem is?"

"No." He closed his eyes. "Don't want to talk."

"What do you want?"

He opened his eyes. "Fuck."

"Fuck? You want to fuck?"

"Want to fuck you."

"That is so... A compliment. That's what it is. I'm complimented that you want to fuck me."

His eyes closed and opened again. She was smiling at him. "You want to fuck me, too?" he asked.

"Ask me when you're sober."

"'Kay."

She slid her hand over his head. It felt good, her palm warm but not too hot. He closed his eyes.

"What kind of help did you need?"

"Wha' help?"

She sighed. It felt like the sound of a southern breeze. A breeze on a dessert island. He could imagine her in a bra and a small dancing skirt like the Hawaiian dancers wore. Her hips moving rhythmically from side to side. Her red hair down. And longer. Maybe down to her waist. Her feet bare.

He'd be in a hammock, and then she would crawl in with him and—

His thoughts were heavy. Weighing too much for his mind to hold on to. Slipping slowly away.

"It's okay." Her voice was low. Melodic. Her hand curled around his fingers.

It was like one of his many dreams of her. He tugged her.

"Come closer," he said.

She laughed softly. "There's no room."

"Make room for you." He shifted to the back cushions, pulling her down to him. His eyes kept wanting to close, but he wouldn't let them. Not until he got what he wanted. What he needed. "We'll just...cuddle."

"You said you wanted my help."

"Can't sleep."

"Why not?"

There was a little frown line between her eyebrows, and he reached up. Slowly because his arm felt so heavy. With the pad of his index finger, he smoothed the line until she stopped frowning. "I need you."

"That's the help you need? A sleeping aid?"

"I hurt." He didn't want to say the words, but they came out anyway.

"Why? Why do you hurt?"

"War. It's terrible."

"It is."

"Why do people kill other people?"

"I don't know, August." Tears formed in her eyes.

"Sleep with me."

As she looked into his eyes, tears slipped down her cheeks. "I don't think we'd be comfortable together."

"The bed." He pushed himself up into a sitting position. *Whoa.* The room whirled, and he sat still.

"Are you okay? Do you feel nauseated?"

He kept looking down, breathing hard until the dizziness stopped. "I'm okay." He got up and kicked over the bucket. His mind was clear enough to be glad that he hadn't thrown up. His stomach felt better now than before.

Because Elle was here with him.

"Bathroom," he said, and swerved into it.

When he came out, she was waiting for him. She reached for him, holding his arm though he told her he didn't need her. That he was okay.

He *was* better, too. Walking almost straight as she steered him into his bedroom. If anyone else walked into his place, he could probably fool them that he was only a little drunk.

This last year, he'd been good at fooling people.

He tumbled into his bed.

"You want me to take off your jeans?" she asked.

"Take off all my clothes," he said.

She laughed and reached to unzip him. She didn't have to unbutton him because he'd left his jeans unfastened, his fingers too clumsy to button up.

He closed his eyes. It felt good to have her

unzip him. And now she was taking off his jeans. Tugging them. Making a little grunting noise because he couldn't help.

He should help, but he was so tired. So heavy.

Then the jeans were off him, and he felt better. Lighter. She turned off the light and crawled into bed with him.

"It's going to be okay," she whispered.

"I know." But she wasn't close enough. She was too far away. He reached for her, shifting to her, spooning her.

"Better," he said. "Much better."

"August, we really shouldn't. We—"

"Shhhh." His eyes closed. It felt so good. It felt so right. It felt...

With a long sigh, she relaxed against him.

He sighed back, falling into sleep, with one last thought in his mind. *Perfect.* That's what it felt like. Perfect.

Thirty-one

Elle woke up slowly. Warm and sweaty, with a man's arms wrapped around her. She knew exactly where she was and whose semi-aroused penis was pushed against her butt.

A big mistake, she told herself. But she closed her eyes and stayed there another minute before inhaling and inching away.

He murmured a protest. She shifted to the edge of the mattress, then rolled off and stood at the side of the bed, gazing at him.

He made another wordless protest, then was silent, though his breaths were heavy. She resisted an urge to pull the thin blue blanket over his arm, and she left him sleeping. Sadness followed her. She used his bathroom, and when she washed her hands, she saw in the mirror that her hair was wild, her face was shiny, and she looked like a woman who'd done more than just fall asleep with a man.

She made a face at her image. She really wanted to live up to the wanton woman in the mirror—but *not* with a man who was sleeping off the effects of a night of drinking.

In the living room, she grabbed her purse and locked the front door before letting herself out. She walked across the grass toward the resort parking lot, where she'd parked her car at the northwest edge. As she neared her car, a red hatchback was turning into the lot. The parking lot was almost full, but there were a couple of empty spots closer to the resort. The car drove past them, as if the driver were heading toward the end.

It pulled into a spot about six parking spaces from Elle's.

She hurried her steps, knowing that it had to be someone who worked at the resort.

The car door opened and closed when she was still about fifty yards from the parking lot, and she saw Melanie, who'd been handling the reception desk with Chuck the day she and Harper had driven here.

Even from this distance, Elle could see Melanie's face light up. Elle groaned. Nothing like a good piece of gossip to liven up a dull day at work. By noon, a big percentage of the Trouble Bay townspeople would know she'd been spotted making the walk of shame from August's chalet early in the morning, along with commentary about her wrinkled clothes and wild hair.

Elle was certain that someone would gleefully tell Lissa, watching her reactions sharply.

That thought wasn't exactly distasteful to Elle.

She smiled and waved at the desk clerk.

The desk clerk smiled back.

By the time Elle reached her car, she was laughing softly.

Still, she needed to talk to August. To warn him.

And they needed to talk about last night.

Her lips turned down. *That* hadn't been funny. No matter what else had happened last night—or what else hadn't happened—August needed professional help.

And not just from anyone. He'd called *her*. He needed *her*. And, damn it, whether he wanted it or not when he was sober, he was going to get her help.

In her car, she pulled down the seat belt. Though she was frowning, anticipation was growing inside her.

When she'd planned this screenwriting getaway with Nate, she had thought it would be an interesting summer. But she'd had no idea *how* interesting...

Thirty-two

August woke up sweaty and alone in his T-shirt and briefs, breathing too hard. He kept his eyes closed. He'd been stinking drunk last night, but not so drunk that he didn't remember calling Elle. Asking her to help him. Not so drunk that he didn't remember that she'd come into his place, and he'd asked her to stay with him for the night. Not just stay in his cottage; but to sleep in his bed.

And she had.

Some of the details slipped away, but he remembered telling her that he hurt.

Like a kid, needing her help again.

He groaned, putting his hands over his face. He smelled his stale whiskey breath. He needed to get up and take a shower and brush his teeth.

He didn't recall that he'd made any moves on her besides sleeping with her. He was grateful for that, because in the shape he'd been in, he would have done a piss-poor job of it.

If he ever made love to her, he wanted it to be spectacular. The best lovemaking she'd ever had, giving her a dozen orgasms as she clutched his shoulders and screamed out his name.

He groaned. Cutting off those thoughts. And as much as he wanted to stay in bed all day, he was already late. He wasn't on a time clock but worked almost every day, usually starting early. If need be, he worked shifts for workers who called in sick. He'd even cleaned when necessary. He didn't enjoy it, but if he didn't, his mother would do it, and he'd done worse things in his life than wield a mean toilet brush.

He never forgot how lucky he was to be part of this place. He never forgot where he'd come from. He never forgot how afraid he'd been that day when he was eight years old, standing in the cold, too scared to even cry, thinking he and his mother might die.

He never forgot that he'd been saved by Elle, a small girl with a big heart.

And look how he'd repaid her.

Making her come over last night.

Dragging her into bed with him.

He pushed himself up and headed to the bathroom for his shower.

Less than a quarter hour later, he was dressed and on the phone as the coffee percolated on his counter.

On the third ring, Elle answered. "Good morning, August."

"I'm sorry about last night."

"We need to talk."

He winced.

"You called me," she said, "asking for help. I didn't call you."

"I was drunk. I'm not normally drunk."

"Aren't you?"

He frowned. Not angry at her. Angry at himself. "Usually I can control it better."

"If it's gotten to the point where you need to control it, then it's a problem."

He closed his eyes. "I'll stop. Right now. I'm not drinking anymore."

She didn't reply.

"What else do you want from me?" His voice had risen, and he got to his feet, spurred by anger at himself. Anger at her because she'd seen him like that. And anger at the world that had random violence and people who thought it was okay to kill other people.

"You called me last night," she said, "and asked me to help you. Last night you were drunk, but today you're sober. Today, I'm saying yes to your plea. Let me help you, August."

"That wasn't a sober request," he said. "You know that."

She didn't reply. He closed his eyes tightly, then opened them.

"I'm fine," he said with more force. "I don't need to talk. I have to go to work now. Thank you for your help. Good-bye."

He hung up. Put the phone on the counter. He had an urge to go in the cupboard where he kept his booze, then grab a bottle and drink. Just him and the bottle as he guzzled it down.

He never drank in the morning. Sometimes he would have a drink in the afternoon. Lately it had been more often. More than he liked to count or remember.

That was just the last few weeks. Before that, he usually had been able to refrain from drinking until the nighttime. Sometimes, he'd skipped a night or two. Telling himself that if he could skip a day, he didn't have a problem.

The past few weeks, that had changed. Lately, he'd been having a few drinks every night. He told himself that summer nights did that to him. And if it helped him not think about what he'd gone through, then what was he hurting?

Now he knew who he was hurting. Himself. His family. Everyone who he came in contact with.

Swearing loudly, he strode to the cupboard. Took out a bottle. Opened it. Then stepped to the sink, upended the bottle, and watched the golden liquid pour into the sink.

After that was empty, he took another bottle out. Poured that out. Then another. And another. And another. And two more.

Then he went to the fridge and found two bottles of beer. He emptied them in the sink, then tossed the bottles into the recycling bin. He felt weakened. Sitting on a kitchen chair, he bent over the table, his elbows on the dark wood, his hands holding his head.

He was unhappy and drinking and cutting himself off from society some. He didn't wake up and crave alcohol, so he was pretty sure he wasn't an alcoholic...yet. But no one started out as an alcoholic. If he kept it up, he didn't know what might happen.

Making sure it wouldn't happen was an easy fix. He would just stop drinking. Right now.

He straightened and stood. Instead, he'd do what he'd always done. What other men, women, and children had done before him and would do after he was long gone. He'd persevere. He'd do all right. He might even learn to appreciate what he had and to enjoy life.

He was just going through a bad patch, and he'd get over it.

No one but Elle would need to know that he'd had a problem.

His phone dinged. Someone texting him. He looked down at it and saw it was from Elle.

Almost forgot. The desk clerk saw me leave this morning. You know what that means.

He groaned. Great. Now the whole damn town would be talking about him and Elle. Because of his call for help, because he'd dragged her into bed with him, people would think she was a tramp. In any other place, that wouldn't matter. But in this small, insulated town, people talked. People judged.

He'd asked her to marry him last night. At least, he thought he had. And she'd said no.

She was right to say no. He wasn't good enough for her.

Thirty-three

Elle looked down at the number on her phone display and grabbed the phone off of the kitchen table she and Nate were using as their desk. "It's my mom."

"Calling from Rome?"

She nodded, glancing at the clock. Nearly ten a.m., which meant it was five p.m. in Rome. "Mom! Hi!"

"Hi, Elle. I heard about last night."

Elle's mouth gaped open.

"Elle? Are you there?"

She nodded, pulling her scattered wits together. "What did you hear?"

"That you spent the night with August. How was it?"

Elle groaned and bent forward, putting her hand on her forehead. "You're calling to ask me the details?"

Her mom laughed heartily. "Not the details. Just the overall effect. You and August. To be honest, I hoped you would get together. So did Duke and Pilar."

"Is *that* why you encouraged me to spend the

summer in Trouble Bay?"

"Silly. I didn't push you into anything. You *wanted* to go. And Duke and Pilar and I didn't think of it just this summer. We've thought that since the day you had Harper."

"I'd just birthed a baby fathered by another man, and you and August's parents were matchmaking?"

"Don't be so prissy. We all could see how good you were together. And now you are."

"I wasn't. We weren't." Her voice rose. "We *aren't*."

"You didn't stay overnight with him?"

She stifled a groan and the urge to punch her fist into the wall. Neither would be productive, and it was possible she could knock a hole in the wall, but more probably she would hurt her hand.

"Mom, just leave it, will you, please? It's none of your business."

A choked laugh came from across the table. She looked at Nate, who was grinning.

On the other side of the phone, there was silence for a moment that had nothing to do with the long-distance connection. "I could never talk to my mother about anything like this," her mom said.

"Mom, there are some things that a mother and daughter shouldn't share."

"I've always been completely open with you."

"Exactly."

There was silence again.

"Too open?" her mom asked.

"Sometimes."

"I thought of you like a girlfriend. A mini me."

"I'm not your girlfriend. I'm your daughter. And I'm not a mini version of you, either."

"Crap. Have I been a bad mom?"

Elle closed her eyes, then opened them, wondering why she'd picked this time to take her mother to task for not being the perfect mother. "You've been a great mom. I don't want you to change. "

"Are you just saying that?"

"I'm not. You're fun and smart, and you've made me *think*. I've always been proud of you." She took a deep breath. "But stay out of my personal life. Okay?"

"I went too far, is that it?"

She smiled. Her mother didn't know how to stop going too far. "I'm a big girl. A mom. If I make any decisions, I'll let you know."

"All right, baby. Just remember that sometimes Mom does know best."

"Mother!"

Laughter came through the phone. "Just kidding. Though in another ten years or so, you'll be telling Harper you know best."

"You think you can make me empathize with your position by pointing out that, in my future, I'll be the mom advising my daughter?"

"Maybe."

Elle easily imagined her mom's grin. "You can't fool a psychologist."

"And you can't fool a mom. You did sleep with August."

"Mom!"

"I have to go soon. Liam and I are off to meet

friends at an art gallery, and then we're going to dinner."

Elle didn't know who Liam was—and she decided that it was better not to know. "Sounds lovely."

"It's very lovely. I'm living my dream right now. I want you to live your dream, too. Can you put Harper on the phone?"

"She's at daycare."

"Would I know her daycare teacher?"

"She's my age. Allison Woodly. She said we're second or third cousins."

"Little Allison? Blond hair and a big smile."

Elle laughed. "Not so little anymore. She's about six inches taller than I am. I think her breasts are thirty-eight D."

"Forty double D," Nate said.

"But she still has that smile," she continued, not looking at Nate. "She has a day care in her home. She's very reasonable, and Harper loves playing with the other kids."

"I'm glad your stay is working out. Especially with August."

"Mom!"

She laughed. "Love you. I've got to go now. Bye."

She hung up before Elle had a chance to reply.

"She heard about you and August." Nate was grinning.

Elle groaned. Of course he'd known about last night's overnight stay. But she'd told him that she'd stayed overnight because August had needed her. Nothing more. He'd nodded, not making any comments or suggesting anything more than friendship was involved.

"Not you, too," she said and heard the whine in her voice. Too bad. She wanted to whine this morning. Whine loudly.

"I went for a walk this morning after you came home." He grinned. "News travels fast here."

She made a face. She would bet that locals who normally didn't step near Lissa's overpriced tourist trap were suddenly shopping there this morning, dropping hints about Elle's overnight stay with Lissa's boyfriend.

"Let's get on with the next scene," Elle said, but she couldn't stop a smile. It was immature and petty of her to enjoy the thought of Lissa's discomfiture, but sometimes immaturity and pettiness were just more fun than being a grown-up.

Thirty-four

When Chuck came for dinner on Thursday, Sylvia wasn't surprised. Chuck lived in the cottage on the Schmidts' estate at the northern end of town. The Schmidts stayed there only a few months out of the year, and he took care of their property year-round for free rent and a small monthly remuneration. It was a step up from living over the Ready to Roar Tavern, which he'd done for a few months. She'd never approved and had worked hard to convince the Schmidts that he was responsible enough to be their caretaker. No one had been happier than her when it turned out that he really was responsible and didn't have wild parties.

Women, yes, but wild parties, no. That was good enough for her. She didn't expect miracles or a saint. In fact, she preferred that he not be a saint, as she did want grandchildren some day. And she was getting to the point where she'd like that someday to be someday soon.

Though he lived elsewhere, he came over to her place for dinner often. She suspected it was to save money, and she was a good cook, but even when she'd been going through her angry and bitter stage of life—a stage that had lasted way too long—she had taken care not to alienate Chuck. Even then she'd known that he might be all she'd have.

She wanted the best for him, and the best wasn't an embittered parent. It had taken her longer to realize that she needed to treat herself with the same kindness she was showing to him.

Tonight he was far from embittered, with a cocky attitude and big smile. She didn't say or ask anything. When he was ready, he would tell her.

Sure enough, it wasn't until he was halfway through her portabella pizza—which he didn't even realize was healthy, just that it tasted delicious—that he spit out his news.

"Guess who asked me out?" Laughter glinted in his eyes.

Her heartbeat quickened. "Elle?"

"Elle Styles? Mom, she's way out of my league."

She stiffened. "Has she said that?"

"Elle? Hell no. She treats me like I'm just as smart as her. As smart as anyone."

"You *are* as smart as anyone."

"Aw, mom. I'm not completely stupid, but I'm no Einstein."

"The only Einstein I ever heard of was Einstein. But I'll tell you what he wasn't."

"What's that?"

"Charles Pascal Jr. That's what Einstein would never be."

He laughed so hard he pounded the table, and Sylvia knew that the two couples staying in the Betsy and William room and the Henry and Louisa room, who were sitting on the front porch, could probably hear his shouts of laughter.

Good. Nothing was better than hearing shouts of laughter. And for her, nothing was better than hearing her son's laughter.

"You should ask her out," she said. "You're handsome, people like you, and you're handy. As for being smart, *I* think you're smart."

Chuck smiled, and it was a sweet smile for a grown man. Surely any woman—no matter how intelligent—would look at his smile and her heart would melt.

"You're the smart one in the family," Chuck said. "Dad was lucky he married you."

Her heart ached a little, because at seven, the age he'd been when his father had been killed, he must have known how often his father stayed out all night. He must have heard her crying. He must have seen her rigid silence as she seethed in anger.

And he must have seen that his father didn't give a damn.

Thinking about it, she didn't regret what she'd done. Not for one second. What she regretted was the necessity. She didn't *want* to be a killer. But sometimes it seemed the best choice. Sometimes the other person just really deserved to die.

Maybe Chuck didn't want to remember the bad times. She didn't fault him for that.

"Any woman would be lucky to marry *you*," she said, happy to change the subject.

"Mom, you're prejudiced."

"I have even more. You're healthy, you're a good worker. You have a *glorious* smile."

"Yeah, that's me." One corner of his mouth tipped down. "No maternal prejudice there."

"Not a bit. That's my completely impartial opinion."

They both grinned, and she bent forward. "So what did I miss while I was busy today?"

"Major gossip."

"You know I don't like gossip. Would you like another Italian sausage?"

"Sure."

She set another sausage on his plate. While he was putting it in the bun, then grabbing the mustard and ketchup, she plunked down and bent toward him. "So what's the gossip?"

He laughed. "I knew you'd ask. Last night Elle stayed over at August's place. The news is probably all over town by now. Hell, you're probably the only one who didn't hear yet."

She shook her head. She'd been busy today with her guests, the usual morning buffet, then cleaning, paying bills, and making b biscuits for tomorrow morning. She'd gotten more calls than usual today, but she'd been too busy to gossip with friends. She'd only picked up calls she didn't know, including two from out of state who were making reservations that filled up August. The others were all locals, and she'd planned to call them back later tonight.

"Mom, you don't look good."

She felt dizzy. Faint. She inhaled deeply and exhaled deeply. Her heart was beating too fast.

Was she having a heart attack? Not now. Oh, God, not now.

"Are you sick? You want me to call nine-one-one?"

She shook her head. "He's dating Lissa. Melanie saw her leaving early this morning. She said Elle's hair was wild, and she was wearing last night's clothes.

"Melanie saw Elle leaving his place this morning. Are you okay?"

"I'm fine. I'm just..." *Sorry.* More sorry than she could tell him. "I just thought that Elle would be good for you."

"Yeah, you've dropped a few hints."

She tried to smile but failed. It was like smiling at the death of her hopes for him and Elle.

"To be honest, Mom, I wouldn't have minded." Chuck shrugged. "I like her. A lot. But I could tell that I didn't have a chance."

She sucked her lower lip in. This was one of those instances where anything she might say would be wrong.

It wasn't easy being a mother.

"I think you have as much of a chance with her as any other man. And if things don't work out with her and August—"

"Mom, you can practically see the sparks going off between them." He frowned at her. "And before you ask, I'm okay with it. I'm good. Real good. Don't you have dessert?"

She got up automatically. She was cutting down on sugar, but she did have a quart of key lime ice cream in her freezer. Maybe tonight, she'd have a bowl. A big bowl. This was a night for ice cream.

In a moment, she brought back two bowls of ice cream. As usual, his had two scoops. As wasn't usual, so did hers.

He dug in, shoving ice cream into his mouth, not looking heartbroken. Not even heart bruised. He just looked like a happy pig in the trough.

She probably looked the same way, shoving spoonfuls of ice cream into her mouth just as fast.

"I didn't tell you the other news." He grinned, a smear of ice cream on the left corner of his mouth.

"What's that?"

"Lissa called me and asked me out." He laughed.

Sylvia pushed away her ice cream, even though she still had a couple spoonfuls left. She'd suddenly lost her appetite.

"Why?" she asked.

"Because I'm so handsome and have such great muscles."

She looked down at her ice cream and felt sick. "She heard the gossip. It's revenge dating."

He shrugged and looked unconcerned. "Yeah, I know."

"Did you say yes?" She vaguely realized she was holding the spoon so tightly that the edge was digging into the pad of her thumb.

"What do you think?"

Unable to reply, she shook her head.

"I said I was busy, and she could call me another night."

Her fingers opened; the spoon dropped onto the floor, bouncing on the tiles.

He bent to pick it up. When he came upright, holding the spoon, he said, "She's a bitch, Mom. Did you really think I'd go out with her?"

Tears started in her eyes. "You're the smartest son in the world."

He laughed at her. Still tearing up, she laughed with him.

Thirty-five

"We didn't do too badly." Elle stood up from the kitchen chair and stretched her back. "Despite all the personal drama."

"For a first day, we did great." Nate's thick, gray eyebrows rose. "You should sleep with a guy more often. Obviously sex increases your productivity."

"There was no sex." She socked him in the fleshy part of his shoulder. "And that was a bad joke."

"Hey." He pulled back, holding his hand over his shoulder. "Those knuckles of yours are sharp."

"My knuckles are my superpower."

"I should warn August."

"Ha ha." She waved her fist in front of his face, and he pretended to cower. Though maybe he was really cowering, and she dropped her hand. "The real reason we're doing so well is because of those story beats of yours."

He shook his head, getting to his feet, too. "You're a natural storyteller. That's why I wanted to make a movie about your dissertation."

"And here I thought it was the salacious subject matter."

"Sex, murder, and dirty politicians." He winked. "Can't go wrong with all of that. We might finish even faster than six weeks."

She grimaced. "It took me more than five years to write the dissertation."

"I can tell you researched very thoroughly."

"I enjoy research, and the subject was interesting." She grinned. "Even though it wasn't all salacious."

He winked. "Enough to make it into a movie."

She opened the fridge and grabbed the pitcher of iced tea and poured herself a glass while Nate headed to the coffeemaker. "There was some true love in my dissertation, too."

"All the best movies need a love story." Standing in front of the coffeemaker on the counter, he wiggled his eyebrows at her. "Real life people need love stories, too."

She gulped down the ice tea, then set the glass on the counter. "I'm going for a walk, then to the sitter's to pick up Harper."

"I'll go for a walk, too. I need the exercise."

She looked at him, a sinking feeling in her belly. She'd walked with him before, but they had different definitions of the word. He strolled. She fast-walked.

He chuckled. "You don't have to look so horrified. I don't plan on walking with you."

"You mean shuffling your feet, don't you?" She smirked. "I don't call that walking."

"You're a mean woman," he said.

She laughed and headed toward the bedroom to put on her sneakers. While she was tying a shoelace, Nate called out that he was leaving. A few seconds later, she heard the screen door clang shut. She grimaced. No doubt he was trying to prove her wrong about his slowness.

Her shoelaces tied, she hurried out of the bedroom, then petted Misty and gave her a treat. While Misty nibbled quickly yet daintily, Elle grabbed her sunglasses and a sunhat.

Leaving the small rental house, Elle headed to Main Street and turned left. There were a lot of tourists, which was good for Trouble Bay. She enjoyed listening to their comments as they stopped in front of a building and read the menu or historic sign, or looked at art works signed by local painters or sculptors or woodcarvers. All the things she was doing, too.

Right now, she had her eye on a brass and wooden TV stand, but she held back. She didn't know what she was going to do in the future or how much money she would be making. She had some ideas of what she wanted to do, but she had a daughter to raise, a cat who liked expensive treats, and a future to take into consideration. She was well aware that her plans weren't as wise as they should be. She should be applying for positions. Instead, she had vague and impractical ideas in her mind.

That was in addition to having wild sex with August. Her number one plan.

When he was sober, of course.

She circled around two couples who were walking slowly. Across the street, she saw a chocolate shop, a pie shop, and a T-shirt shop. She shouldn't do it, but she headed for the chocolate shop. Dark chocolate was healthy, after all. So were nuts. All of that much make her very healthy.

When she stepped into the shop, there was a line already. Obviously she wasn't the only one in search of health foods, she told herself, snickering silently at her joke.

And then she clearly heard the words coming from the beginning of the line. "She did the walk of shame already," a woman's voice said.

"What was she wearing?"

"According to Melanie, whatever she was wearing, it looked like she'd been sleeping in it."

"Really?" The other voice trilled with delight as Elle stood frozen.

Of course, she knew about it. Nate had told her. And she didn't hadn't planned to let it hurt her.

"Really." The first voice was familiar. "Melanie said it looked like she and August had done the down-and-dirty dance all night long."

There was tittering. Standing frozen in line, Elle realized that the reason she could hear so clearly was that everyone had stopped talking to listen to the two women. If they were worried that the children would hear something they shouldn't, they didn't say anything to shut up the gossips.

And they were talking about someone—*her*—that most of the people didn't even know.

What was wrong with people?

"I wonder what Lissa and her parents will say."

"You think they'll know?"

"Really? By now the whole town will know."

The two women laughed. Elle turned and headed out of the chocolate shop, the bell ringing behind her. She'd known this would happen. She'd even laughed at the thought.

Now that it had happened in front of her, it wasn't funny anymore.

The hell of it was that she craved chocolate more now than before. She could eat a whole pan of brownies herself. And she wouldn't share.

Let them talk, she thought. Let them think what they will.

After all, if she had a chance to sleep with August—*really* sleep with him—she would grab it. Naked. Sweaty. Non-sleeping.

Yes, he had problems, but she'd worry about that later.

Marching now, she headed to the end of the street where there was a bakery, and hopefully no one would be gossiping about her, because she really wanted a brownie now.

"I think the whole town will know," the woman had said.

As she fast-walked around tourists—because the brownies wouldn't wait for her forever—she wondered about another question one of the women had asked.

What will Lissa and her parents say?

Despite her discomfort, she couldn't stop a smile...and then a chuckle.

What *would* they say?

Thirty-six

August headed into the Mystical Bakery on a whim. Though he had a sweet tooth, he normally didn't stop off at bakeries. Maybe it was because he'd promised Elle he wouldn't drink. He was keeping his promise, and if he couldn't have alcohol, he would damn well have one of the best brownies in the town of Trouble Bay.

As he opened the door, the bell above the entranceway dinged. There was a line of four women, and one man was off to the side, checking out the glass-enclosed shelves. August stepped to the end of the line. He was well acquainted with the candy choices, and knew what he wanted. The first woman in line was a blond wearing a pale blue sundress with short sleeves and casual canvas shoes, her wavy hair almost reaching her shoulders.

"What's your rule for the day, Sylvia?" the store clerk asked.

Chuck's mom, August thought. From the back, it was hard to tell her age, but she was a classy woman.

The bell rang, someone else coming in.

"My rule for the day is one that I try to remember every day," Sylvia said. "And I'll take two chocolate caramel truffles."

"Good choice. And what rule is that?"

"My number one rule—love thyself."

Behind August, someone gasped, and he stiffened, recognizing the sound and the woman who made it. He took a deep breath as Louise, the co-owner of the bakery, spotted him and the woman behind him, her eyes sharpening.

Love thyself, he thought. Better yet, love they neighbor. And right now, that sounded pretty damn good.

He turned and looked behind him at Elle, a crooked *oh crap* smile on her face, as though she wanted to be anywhere but here.

Not him. Her face was water to his parched eyes. He didn't need alcohol. Just looking at her made him feel light-headed. And the need to hop into bed with her that he'd had last night was back again. This time, sleeping wasn't on his mind.

"Funny seeing you here," he said.

"Nothing funny about it. I only go to the best places." She took a small step sideways, looking forward. "Right, Sylvia?"

Sylvia turned. "Absolutely. I've never been disappointed at Louise and Sally's place."

"That's our number one rule," Louise called out in her rusty voice. "Never disappoint."

"An excellent one," Sylvia said, still looking at Elle. "What's your rule?"

"I'm not big on rules, but I did have one that was broken today."

"And what's that?"

Tension hummed in the store. August narrowed his eyes.

"I had an unspoken rule that the whole town wouldn't talk about me at least until the third week I was here." She lifted her hand in a throwaway gesture. "But that's pretty much out the window."

Sylvia's jaw dropped. August felt as if he'd been slammed by a giant fist in his belly.

A chuckle started from the front. Another chuckle started, and another from the two women standing in front of August. They were tourists and probably didn't know for sure what they were laughing about but were smart enough to figure it was about gossip about him and her.

Elle looked up at him, her blue eyes sparkling with laughter. The tightness in his gut loosened, and the anger he'd been holding on to melted away, like water in his ear after swimming. Gone. An invisible weight falling off his shoulders.

He still didn't laugh. He just stared at her. If they'd been alone, he might have fallen to his knees on the ground, then wrapped his arms around her legs, put the side of his face against her thighs, and held on tightly.

Instead, he swallowed and turned around.

Behind him, in line again, Elle told Sylvia that maybe they could get together sometime. Sylvia agreed and said she needed to get home. Then she left, the door closing behind her with another ding. And he looked down at Elle, and his mind went blank.

She smiled at him. "The line's moving."

He should turn and step forward, but instead, he remained standing there, staring at her. "I'm sorry," he said. "I didn't think. I'll tell everyone the truth."

"But the truth is so much more boring than the fantasy." Her voice was low, so only he could hear. She raised her hand and laid it alongside his face, her fingertips at the top of his cheekbone. "I have a better idea. How about if we make it the truth?"

Thirty-seven

His breath stopped in his lungs for an instant as he stared into her blue eyes. Then he exhaled, his heart thumping.

"Outside," he said, his voice as low as hers had been.

Her hand slid off his face, slowly, and he thought she might make love the same way. Slowly.

Bad thoughts. Very bad thoughts.

"Can't I get my brownies first? I could really use one."

"No."

Her eyebrows rose, and she set her lips together, but they curved up at the corners as she strode past him. He followed her, and it was not a chore, walking behind her, checking out the way she walked with her head high, her shoulders straight, her hips in motion.

Right now, he would follow her anywhere.

They walked in silence to the end of the block, when she stopped and waited for him.

"Where are we going?" she asked.

"My car."

"Sounds promising."

He laughed. "You're killing me."

"Killing you is *not* my intention."

His car was on the end of the side street, a block from Bay Street that was busy with mostly tourists and a few natives.

Someone would see them. He knew that. *Someone* would tell everyone else in town.

Right now, he didn't give a damn.

He opened the passenger door for her. "Get in."

"You're pretty bossy." She gave him a twisted smile. "You always this way when you miss your chocolate?"

"Get in."

She got in, her eyebrows up. She was probably picturing him in her mind the way he'd been last night. Drunk and needy.

He was still needy, but he was sober enough now to hide it, even with his nerves tightly stretched.

He slid in the driver's seat and started the car. He drove slowly until he was out of town, then took the shoreline road. He didn't go far before he reached the summer home of two stockbroker friends who weren't coming to town until July. He turned into their driveway and parked at a spot where they could see the lake waters that flowed into the bay. The day was sunny, the water blue. People fishing, boating, kayaking, or sailing. It was still early in the season and not as hot as it would be in July and August. A perfect day.

"So," she said, "did you bring me here to seduce me?"

He sighed and looked at her bright blue eyes and her smile that was mocking him, her cheeks pushed up. "I want to. But not like this."

Her smile turned down. Her cheeks flattened. Her eyes warmed with concern. With caring.

"I'm broken," he said.

She made a wordless cry and leaned toward him. Then she looked down. "Stupid seat belt," she said and unclicked it. She looked up at him, and he could see the sympathy in her eyes.

He winced. *Sympathy* was not what he wanted from her. But what the hell did he expect when he'd told her he was broken? How dramatic could he be?

"It's your time in the Marines," she said. "Not Lissa, right?"

He laughed harshly. "It's not fair to Lissa, but she means nothing to me. I doubt I mean much to her, either. I doubt anyone does, except herself." He grimaced. "And that doesn't say a lot for me."

"August." Her voice was anguished.

He shook his head. "I'm not fishing for sympathy. I just thought you deserved to know the truth."

She touched his arm, not saying a word.

"Yeah, it's my service." He heard the roughness of his voice. The anger. The sadness.

He didn't want to do this, but he forced himself to continue. "The hell of it is that I wasn't even in any action. I worked in FOB. Headquarters. No battles for me." He took a shaky breath. "But I still saw things that made me sick for the human race."

She made a soft cry in her throat and pulled her hand from his arm.

He glanced down and saw that his fists were curled on his thighs. "I'm not talking about fellow Marines, either. Just what man does to man, and man does to woman."

She twisted and pushed herself up on the seat and closer to him, then slid her hand over his shoulders. Not saying anything but giving him silent sympathy and encouragement that he could feel even without looking directly at her.

"The worst part"—his voice broke, and he swallowed before continuing—"is what man does to children."

"Tell me about it."

He frowned. "It's bad."

"Tell me. I can take your pain. You'll feel better."

"It was a bomb in the city." He closed his eyes. "Women and children killed for no reason I could see. It was carnage."

"Why?" Her voice caught, and she swallowed, then asked in a stronger voice, "*Why?*"

"Because we were there. Because they were serving us food, and we were paying for it." He shook his head. "They killed them because of us."

"That's not true. They killed them because of their callousness and their heartlessness."

"If we hadn't been there—"

"You can't blame yourself. You can't blame the Marines."

His jaw clenched. He couldn't look at her. Not yet. He could only listen.

"It wasn't the first time a senseless murder happened." Her voice was quiet, her tone firm. "This goes back to Chicago, doesn't it?"

He closed his eyes now.

"To the night your friend was killed. Rick. Your mom told my mom about him."

He fought tears that burned beneath his eyelids. When he spoke, his voice was thick. "I always wondered why him? It could so easily have been me. Death is so random."

"It's random, but it didn't happen because you were there. It would've happened if you were half a world away."

He half turned to her. "I know you're right, and that it wasn't my fault."

"In your mind you know that..." She shook her head, her smile sad. "But in your heart, you're taking the blame."

"I don't think so. In my heart, I'd rather the children and their mother have lived than me."

She made another sound that was like a cry. "I hope the people who killed them go to a special place in hell."

He closed his eyes that were moistening again. "Jesus, I'm a pussy."

There was a movement on the seat next to him, and he heard her breaths come closer. He opened his eyes and turned slightly. She had scrambled to her knees, and as he watched, she leaned forward, put her arms around him, and hugged him, her left breast against his arm, her head resting on the front of his chest.

He should push her away. Tell her he didn't need this.

Instead, he closed his eyes again, his arms at his side, and they remained like that in the car, the sun's rays warm through the window, and he breathed in her scent that made him think of marshmallow Easter bunnies, the yellow, blue, and pink kinds. Sweetness tripled.

Finally, he opened his eyes, turned, and put his arms around her. She gripped his back, and they both held on to each other tightly. As if they never wanted to let the other go. At least, that's how he felt, with his throat full of tears and sadness, and maybe something more.

Healing.

Maybe.

Love.

Yes.

Because he did love her. He'd loved her since he was eight, and she'd saved him and his mother.

And now she was saving him again.

Minutes passed before she moved, and he realized the position was awkward for her. He slowly pulled back, and she shifted to her seat.

"Is that how you treat all your patients?" he asked.

"Just the handsome ones."

He shouldn't want to smile, but he did. "Yeah? That's the only qualification?"

"It helps if they were there when I had my baby."

"That narrows it down."

"And if I want to make love to them. So far, only one guy has qualified."

He looked at her for a moment, feeling his smile slip away.

"I'm not good enough for you. Not yet."

She opened her mouth, and he shook his head, cutting off her objections. "I don't want to come to you this way," he said, "with need and weakness. I want to come to you with strength."

"Have you thought that if you're afraid of showing weakness, you'll never be strong?"

"That sounds like one of those Zen riddles that never make sense."

"It makes sense to me. Fear of weakness is a *fear*. That makes fear your weakness. This isn't about fear or strength. This is sex." She looked down, a vertical line indenting between her eyebrows. "Sex is just...sex. Wonderful sex, I hope, but in the end, it's just two people making each other feel really good."

"I want to agree with you." He put his hand on the side of her wild hair. "But I can't. For you it may be just sex. For me with you...it will be much more. I'm not ready to take that step. Not now."

She looked away. "You should talk to someone about this."

"I just did."

"I can't promise to be there for you when you're ready."

There was silence for a moment. Outside the car, birds chirped, a breeze shook the leaves of the oak tree nearest them. He even heard the faraway voices from the lake.

But between them was dead silence. Dead air.

"I'll have to take that chance," he said.

"I don't even know how long I'll be here. Nate and I just rented the house for six weeks."

"Are you giving me a timeline?"

"A countdown for sex?" She smiled. "I'll tell you what. I'll give you a timeline for brownies. If I can't have sex, I'm damn well having brownies."

He started the car. "So brownies are second best?"

"I haven't had sex with you yet. Brownies might be first best."

He laughed loudly. "Now I'm scared."

"You should be very scared. I like brownies a lot."

He looked at her. And in that second, he wanted her badly. He wanted her more than he'd ever wanted a woman.

But he took a breath. Not now. Not this moment.

"When we make love," he said, because it would be making love with her, not sex, "it will be amazing."

Her eyes widened, and he smiled slightly, then backed up the car. As he neared the road, he realized he didn't feel broken anymore. Bruised still, but not broken.

Thirty-eight

"People are talking about you," Nate said in the easy chair across from her in the rented house, Misty draped across his lap as he petted her. It was dusk outside, the sky gray and slowly getting darker. The front and back doors were open, no need for air conditioning yet. The screen doors kept the bugs out and let the fresh air in.

Her legs stretched out on the hassock, Elle set down her tablet as she listened to the male crickets chirp outside and the frogs croak. Hoping to attract a mate. She wished them better luck than she'd had this afternoon.

"Nice for them," she said. "Gives them something to do."

He laughed. "You don't care?"

"Nope."

"So, you don't plan to live here?"

"Maybe I do plan on living here."

"With Mr. Sexy?"

She grinned. "You think he's sexy, too? I didn't know you ran that way."

"Not me." He held up his hands. "I have my own sexy lady in my sights."

"Really?" She leaned forward. "And who would that be?"

"She would be none of your business."

"You tell me yours. I'll tell you mine."

"What is this? Eighth grade?"

She laughed. "I like it here. I don't know why it doesn't bother me that people are talking about me. Maybe because I lived in a bigger city."

"Maybe because you do plan on sleeping with him."

"Maybe that's it. Maybe I'm just well adjusted."

"I like my take better."

"Maybe because you're a man, and men always have to have the last say."

Misty meowed—as if in agreement—and in one limber move that a ballet dancer would enjoy, pushed up to her four feet and jumped to the floor. Her tail waving, she sauntered out of the room.

"The last say?" Nate asked. "Looks to me as if the cat just had the last say. For sure, you're not talking about me."

She made a face at him because he was right— this time. She was a teensy bit upset about August's decision. All she'd wanted to do was to have sex. It wasn't a commitment. She might not even stay in Trouble Bay.

Goose bumps rose on her upper arms, and she crossed her arms and rubbed them. Time to change the subject. "I've been putting it off, but I need to start applying for jobs."

He shook his head, his expression sympathetic. "I can remember when I realized I wouldn't make a living that I could depend on as a screenwriter. I always hated the J-O-B word.

But I think we might have a winner with our screenplay. A big one. I've done well with a couple screenplays, and a couple others were flops. But this one...you never know for sure, but I think it has it all."

"Lying and cheating politicians and their wealthy backers," she said.

"And sex." He grinned. "Don't forget the sex."

She grinned back but turned it into a grimace. "I hope you're right. If it is, I'll be glad for both of us. But I can't see this as a career for me. This will be a one-off."

"You're a natural storyteller."

"When I was a kid, I wrote stories. But I don't think I have the passion to make this a career. Not now, anyway. Later maybe. I have a daughter to raise now."

"Are you thinking of teaching? University level?"

She wrinkled her nose. "I've had enough of university. I'd like to go out in the real world and see how that works."

"The real world's a scary place."

She thought of August talking about the children and women who were killed. She swallowed to clear her throat before she spoke. "There's a psychiatric hospital in Green Bay."

"A psychiatric hospital? Wouldn't that be for hardcore cases?" He frowned, his expression serious.

"Possibly. Or there's a prison."

"A lot of plot ideas there," he said.

"Or sad stories."

"Stories of stupidity."

"*Everyone* has stories of stupidity."

He laughed.

"Or I could be a psychologist for regular schools."

He shook his head. "Lousy pay."

"But I'd have summers off to be with Harper. I think." She made a face. "I don't even know if they're hiring psychologists. The way they keep cutting school budgets, I'm not sure if they still have them."

"And think of all that paperwork and red tape."

She made another face. There was always paperwork, but schools were the worst. Then she bit her lip. "Or..."

"Aha!" he said when she didn't continue. "You do have something up your sleeve."

"I was thinking of a woman's wellness group."

"Where?"

"Here." She swept her arm out. "Trouble Bay."

"For locals?"

"Of course. Not during the tourist season. The locals are too busy, especially in summer. It would be something for the women during the other nine months of the year."

"You could be with Harper during the summer," he said.

She nodded enthusiastically. Probably too enthusiastically. "I can easily find a place to rent."

"Not a bad idea. I can see only one problem."

"What's that?"

"It's the gossip. Now the ladies of Trouble Bay think you're a slut."

Her jaw dropped open. "Really, Nate? *Really*?"

"Really." He nodded sagely, though his eyes twinkled. "If you really want to do this, I guess you'll have to marry August."

"You know what? I don't want to do the wellness group that much." She was so angry it was hard to enunciate the words. Hard not to shout them out. She didn't know why. Maybe later she would see the humor in this. Much later, when she wasn't shaking inside with anger. "I don't have to make any decisions yet. Right now, the only fiction I want to create is the screenplay."

"You're sure?"

"Absolutely sure."

Thirty-nine

"I'd like to talk to you." Sylvia stood in her kitchen, the phone against her ear. It had been over a week since she'd first talked to Nate in the grocery store. A week of disappointments and bad news.

"Talk?" Nate Finkelstein's low, resonating voice held humor. "I thought you didn't want to see me."

Sylvia looked out at the white, green-roofed, four-car garage in her backyard. Not attached, of course. They didn't attach garages in the mid-nineteenth century. No wonder people either called her three-storied bed-and-breakfast *quaint* with a dreamy smile or *old-fashioned* with a sour face.

Right now, she was having a sour-face moment. "Excuse me, but where did that come from?"

"You broke our date a week ago."

"I had a leak in my kitchen sink. That wasn't a broken date. That was an emergency." She enunciated each word clearly to keep from raising her voice. What was wrong with men and their fragile egos?

"Really? You really had a leak?"

"Of course, I had a leak." She didn't hold back the irritation in her voice. "If I didn't want to date you, I would have said so. I don't need to make excuses."

"Well... In that case, my apologies."

"What makes you think I would do something like that?"

"Because you're a beautiful, young shiksha, and I'm a short, old Jew with bushy eyebrows and a nose like a bugle."

There was silence on the other end of the phone.

"You're not saying anything?" he asked.

She thought she heard nervousness in his voice, and it made her smile. "I was just thinking..."

"This is starting to sound dangerous."

She laughed, the anger she'd been feeling when she'd called him oozing out of her. He'd made her laugh in the grocery store, and that hadn't changed. She was glad for it. She didn't have a lot of humor in her life, and she knew it was her own fault. People looked at her and got serious.

Except for Nate. As if he knew that what she needed was humor.

"Not too dangerous," she said, "but you could trim your eyebrows."

"Or you could do it for me."

"Please, no. We're not on eyebrow-trimming terms yet."

"What terms are we on?"

"I believe you owe me a dinner."

"And dancing."

"And dancing," she said, and felt happy. Then she remembered her wedding, dancing with Charley, all eyes on her. Feeling like Cinderella.

And then Charley had gotten drunk. At least he hadn't made out with her maid of honor at the wedding. He and Nancy had waited until she was pregnant with Chuck.

She forced herself not to grimace. "We can do that another time. I really want to talk with you. Are you available tonight?"

"You ate already?"

"Yes." Of course she had eaten. It was nearly seven. She'd washed dishes and had taken a walk. Then she'd stopped by Trouble Bay Candy and Stationery.

What she'd heard there had made her so furious...

Furious enough to make her hurry home and pick up the phone and call Nate at the number he'd given her.

"I'll come over now," he said. "Maybe I can take you to the ice cream shop."

She rolled her eyes but couldn't stop herself from smiling as she agreed, then hung up.

He really wanted to date her after all.

When he hadn't called back after her plumbing disaster, she'd decided that he wasn't interested.

How silly to think she would use leaky pipes as an excuse to break a date with him. Men were too sensitive.

If she hadn't wanted to go out with him, she would have said no when he asked her. As simple as that. She was at the age where she didn't pretend anymore. The No Excuses Age.

She hurried to inspect her hair and quibble over whether she should change her top. She was wearing her blue skirt, but she thought he would appreciate the red top. She'd heard somewhere that it was scientifically proven that men were attracted to women wearing red. Red stood out. Red was vibrant and sexy—even though she felt neither.

Fifteen minutes later, she was walking away from her house, arm in arm with him, wearing her red top and blue skirt. Not for him. For herself. And she'd changed her sandals for tennis shoes that were comfortable for walking.

She wasn't sure how much men liked tennis shoes, but her feet certainly preferred them.

"It's about Elle," she said, getting to the point. Because Elle was the real reason she'd called him. "It's been almost a week, and there's still talk going around about her night with August. I'm sure it's being kept alive by Lissa Morgan's family."

He snorted.

She glanced over at him, and his lips were twisted in disdain. She stiffened. "I'm sure you're not used to this gossip—"

"If there's one constant in life," he interrupted, "it's gossip. When I lived in Los Angeles, there was more gossip than blades of grass. In fact, a hell of a lot of people in L.A. make a living out of gossip."

"Well..." She gestured dismissively. "That's California."

"It's also university life. In every subject, too. No one wants to see other people do better than they do. Even husbands and wives working in the same field will shred their spouses like they were mozzarella cheese sprinkled on top of a pizza."

"Pizza topping?"

"Hey." He spread his hands out. "I'm a writer."

She laughed, some of the tension easing out of her. "I hope you're not putting *that* in your screenplay."

He chuckled. "I guess that was pretty awful."

She lifted an eyebrow. He *only* guessed?

"Why are you so concerned about Elle?" His expression sobered, and his steps slowed, his face turned to her, his eyes looking straight into hers as if he were trying to see into her mind.

But that would never happen. She broke their gaze, looking straight ahead. Someone had to look straight ahead, or they might step into traffic and be run over by a tourist.

"Are you related to Elle?" he asked.

She stopped at the street corner behind a group of tourists who were trying to figure out where they should go next, not caring that they were holding anyone else up.

"As far as I know, we aren't related. I just admire her spunk. I have since she was a child."

"Spunk." He nodded. "I like that word. It should be used more often. And you're right, it does fit Elle."

The tourists finally moved to cross the main street. The ice cream shop was on this side of the street, and Nate hooked his arm through hers and steered her around the tourists and across the street.

Stepping up to the curb, he said, "You have spunk, too."

She felt as if a jolt of electricity had slammed through her. "That's the nicest thing anyone has ever said to me."

"You're a beautiful woman. Many men must have told you that."

She shrugged. "I would be lying if I said I didn't appreciate that my appearance is pleasing to the eye. But it's not something I earned or strove for. My appearance comes from genetics. But spunk..." She swallowed, because it hurt to think of the years when she didn't have spunk. Years when she'd been pitifully in love with a man with no morals and no heart, until she'd realized he didn't deserve her love. "It took work to get my spunk on."

"Good for you." He said it softly. Sincerely.

Her heart melted a little. This man with his big nose and his odd sense of humor knew how to make a woman feel good.

He made her realize it had been a long time since she'd had a lover.

"You know this town better than I do," he said, his voice brisker. "But I don't know what we can do about the gossip. I think we should ignore it."

She kept walking, facing forward. *I will not hit him.*

Definitely, I will not kill him.

"You don't understand. This is a *campaign* against Elle."

"A campaign? That sounds ominous."

"It is ominous." The indignity of it caused her voice to rise unattractively, but she didn't care. "It shouldn't last this long or have turned nasty. I'm certain that Lissa Norman and her mother are involved." Her eyes narrowed, and she turned to him, her steps slowing. "And very possibly Lissa's father. John is the one with the brains in his family. I know he wants Lissa to marry August. She's almost thirty, and they're probably worried that she hasn't found a man who they consider worthy of her."

"Considering August's heritage, I'm impressed that her parents want him as a son-in-law so badly."

"I'm not a betting woman"—she started walking again—"but if I were, I'd say that money trumps heritage."

"August has money?" Nate's eyebrows rose, like two climbing caterpillars.

"Duke adopted him when he married his mother. They have no other children. Everyone in town knows that August will inherit."

"This gets better all the time." He laughed. "Good for him. I knew he worked for a stepfather, but I hadn't realized there were no other children. I didn't know he was adopted."

She inhaled deeply. It had never bothered her that Chuck was left out in the cold. She might be a murderer, but she wasn't greedy.

"So now you understand?" she asked.

"Sure, I understand. But I still don't know what I should do."

"You're the storyteller. What would you do if this was a screenplay you were writing?"

"Well, for one, I don't think talking to Elle would do any good."

She nodded her agreement.

"I think," he said slowly, "that if we told Elle about the gossip, she would flat-out refuse to change in any way."

"The same with August. He's stubborn that way."

"What this plot needs is a red herring."

"A red herring?" She halted and pointed at a blue door. "Here's the ice cream shop."

He stopped, too, but kept his gaze on her as a family of four passed them on the sidewalk. "Hitchcock always had red herrings in his films. Something to divert attention and to shake things up."

"And what would that red herring be?"

"Someone you know."

"I know everyone. Not counting the tourists."

"Someone closer to you. Very close. And very attractive."

"I don't..." She felt a sinking in her belly and put her hand over her stomach. "You're not talking about Chuck, are you?"

"Would that be so horrible?"

Horrible? No, it was what she'd hoped for but thought it would never happen. "Chuck and Elle? I—"

He was shaking his head, still smiling. And that sinking feeling in her belly tightened.

"Not Chuck and Elle," he said. "Chuck and *Lissa.*"

She stared at him. He took her arm and steered her into the ice cream parlor.

"You need ice cream. Once you have ice cream, everything is better."

Forty

The door to August's office opened, and he looked up from an invoice from their local winery to Chuck in his tan slacks and white short-sleeved shirt that he wore at the reception desk.

"Hey, dude," Chuck said. "Got a moment?"

August leaned back in his chair, glad for the break. "Sure." He gestured to the chair in front of his desk. "Grab a seat."

Chuck sat with his legs apart, hunched over a little and frowning, which wasn't like him. "I have a question."

August nodded, seeing Chuck's discomfort that didn't match his usually easy-go-lucky disposition.

"My mom's kind of got a thing about Elle."

August sat up straight. "Huh?"

"Nothing kinky or weird." Chuck held out his hands as if warding off something bad. "It's just that even when Elle was a kid, she would say that Elle looked so happy that it made her feel happy."

"She's right. That was Elle." Sitting back, August narrowed his eyes. "It's still Elle."

"Yeah, Elle's special. But now this thing has happened."

"What thing?"

"C'mon, you know that thing." Chuck's eyes squinted. "That thing about you and Elle spending the night together. It's still going around town. It just doesn't go away."

August didn't reply right away. His brain felt numb.

Chuck sat back and watched him, not saying anything else. Waiting for August. He looked like he was going to wait all day.

"I don't want to talk about it," August said finally.

Chuck nodded, but he didn't get up. Didn't leave. Instead, he hooked his right leg over his left knee at the ankle. "Kind of easy for you to say. No one's calling you a tramp."

August clamped his teeth together.

"You're not the one getting flack for it," Chuck continued.

"Who's calling her a tramp?" August's fingers curled into fists.

"Now you sound pissed."

"Who is it?"

"They're not saying it to her face, if that makes you feel better. Just behind her back."

"Chuck, that doesn't make me feel better."

"Well, you can't hit anyone, because my mom thinks the people who are keeping the tramp talk alive are Lissa and her mom."

August sat still, thinking, taking it all in. Of course it would be Lissa and her mother.

"So, my mom says I could help."

August just looked at Chuck, who nodded, seeming to take August's silence for affirmation to continue instead of shutting up and leaving.

"She said I have two choices. My mom and that old guy working with Elle already talked about it. The first choice is that I get to be the diversion." He sat back and waited for August's reaction.

After a moment of silence, August said, "You're going to be the diversion."

"Yes." Chuck's eyes lit up, clearly pleased that August understood. "The old guy thinks I should date Lissa. You know. So if she's happy dating me, she's not going to be gossiping about you and Elle." He grinned. "And if Lissa is dating me, people will be talking about us instead of you and Elle."

"You think that's a good idea?" August asked.

"I'm not sure. Tell you the truth, I like the other idea better."

August stiffened. He had the feeling that he wasn't going to like this.

"My mom thinks I should ask Elle out, and then people won't talk about you and her."

"They'll talk about you and Elle instead."

Chuck's right eye squinted. "Hey, are you mad that I'm consulting with you about this?"

Consulting? Maybe he should give Chuck a raise.

Or maybe he should fire him.

"I'm not mad. Go on."

"My mom and I talked about it. I don't plan to do anything that will make people talk about Elle. I'll treat her like she's a lady."

August nodded. "So what have you decided?"

"I haven't decided. I thought I'd run it by you. What do you think?"

He didn't answer right away, because what he thought was that he was angry. Angry enough to do something stupid. And when he'd done stupid in the past, the outcome never worked in his favor.

"I think..." He took a deep breath. "You need to let it go."

Chuck frowned. "What do you mean, let it go?"

"Not interfere. The gossip will die off. Lissa and I are no longer seeing each other. We haven't seen each other for a couple of weeks. If you want to date her, I would have no objection."

"And Elle?" A lock of Chuck's thick blond hair curled down on his forehead, and he pushed it back. "You have no objection there, either?"

August just stared at him a moment. Finally, he said, "I think she's getting talked about enough already. If you go out with her, there will just be more talk, and I wouldn't like that."

"I understand." Chuck unhooked his foot from his knee, then stood. "I'm smarter than people think. What you really just said there was that you didn't care if I date Lissa, but you would care if I dated Elle." He shrugged. "So I won't date her. But, dude..."

"What?" August picked up a pencil. Chuck was right. He was smarter than August had thought, and August had always thought that Chuck was smarter than anyone gave him credit for.

"If you don't want anyone to date her, you'd better claim her for yourself."

As August watched Chuck leave, he took the pencil in both his hands, not even thinking, and broke it in half.

Forty-one

Another week passed. When August walked in town, he paid attention to the snickers of the biggest gossips. He noticed that he was watched by the non-gossips, too. The way they watched him, as if trying to see if there were any signs on him of what he'd been up to and who he'd been with.

It bothered him. Like a mosquito that wouldn't go away, and every time he tried to swat it, the damn thing would zip away, and he could swear it was laughing at him.

It was the last week of June, and August went into town a few times, though he avoided stopping off at the bars.

And he avoided going to the house where Elle was staying. It was harder to stay away from her, which meant he wasn't addicted to booze. Not yet, anyway. He suspected he'd been on the road to getting there.

But Elle... He feared he was already at the addict stage. He'd seen Elle only a few times since they were adults. But they were *memorable* times, every one. And since she'd come to Trouble Bay this summer, at night he would look outside at the boats and the laughing families and the lightning bugs, and he would think that he could pick up the phone and she would come.

Yet he never picked up the phone. He never asked her to come.

But the *wanting* to call her, to see her, to hear her and, oh, God, to touch her, was an ache in his chest.

In the nighttime, he stayed home. He worked hard, from early in the morning and sometimes until late at night. He still walked his parents' dog, and he ate dinner at their house on Thursdays, when Duke made ribs, and his mother made her from-scratch chocolate cake with cherries and an éclair pudding between layers.

On this last week of June, five women came to the resort for the weekend, and two of them were all over him every time he saw them. They were attractive and about his age. He was impressed by their bodies in their shorts and their tiny tops. And their bright smiles. All women looked better with bright smiles. But the women in this group were tall, too, one a blond, one with black hair, and three were brunettes. No redheads on the short side to remind him of Elle.

On the last night of their stay, the blond and one of the brunettes told him they were ready for a rodeo.

He turned them down.

An hour later, he saw Chuck heading to the elevator with the brunette and the blond hanging on his arms.

August dropped his parents' dog at their house, then went back to his chalet and sat outside for a long time, looking at the stars in the sky.

He wasn't sorry he'd said no to them.

Neither one was the woman he wanted to be with.

The ache inside of him, as if a piece of his heart was missing, had been there for too long. At his chalet, he picked up the phone, punched in a phone number, then stepped out on the concrete patio behind the kitchen and sat on a lawn chair to watch the sunset. The phone rang twice, then a woman answered.

"August!" Worry sharpened Sylvia's voice. "Are you calling about Chuck? Is anything wrong?"

He held back a snort. He certainly wasn't going to talk to Chuck's mother about what her son was probably doing right now with the two attractive women. "As far as I know, Chuck is fine. I'm calling about Elle. A week ago, Chuck told me the gossips were still talking about Elle. Has that changed?"

"Don't you know that dalmatians don't change their spots?"

"I've never heard that a dalmatian slandered other dogs."

"The bitches in the canine world," Sylvia said, her tone tart, "are much more pleasant than the bitches in the human world. And I'll have you know that I'm including men in that category."

"She's still being slandered then. You still believe that the people behind this are the Normans?"

"Yes." She spoke forcefully. "They have a lot of influence in town. A lot of followers."

He scowled. "John Norman is bombastic and self-important."

"Janet Norman isn't any better," Sylvia said. "Janet loves being the richest woman in Trouble Bay."

He rubbed his chin. "Duke likes to say that Janet Norman has more jewelry than brains."

"Your father is an astute judge of character." Sylvia made a huffing sound. "But not everyone shares his values. Some ignorant people are impressed by snobbishness and bad manners."

He narrowed his eyes. "The town meeting tomorrow...is that still on?"

"After the two fires last Fourth of July, the sheriff insists that his deputies talk to any locals who will come to the meeting."

"Who's in charge?"

There was a moment of silence. "Angela and I are in charge."

"After the deputies are done, I want to talk."

There was another moment of silence, and for a few seconds, he wondered if they'd lost the connection. Then she spoke. "Angela and I are expecting a big turnout. Do you want us to let people know that you'll be speaking?"

"Yes."

"Including Elle?"

"Including Elle," he said.

"And Lissa and Janet Norman? I'm sure they weren't planning to come."

"The Normans, also. You'll get the message out?"

There was another pause before she spoke again. "You know what you're doing?"

"No, but I'm doing it anyway."

"I can't stop you from doing anything foolish. You're a man, after all. I'll see you tomorrow night."

As she hung up, he thought he knew exactly what he was doing. One of two things. He was going to be a white knight.

Or he was going to be a total ass.

He linked his hands behind his head and looked up at the stars. Anything could happen tomorrow night. Bad or good. The one thing that wasn't going to happen was that he would back down.

Forty-two

It was mid-morning, and Elle and Nate were sitting at the kitchen table, disagreeing about a plot point, when Elle's phone rang. She picked it up, as she did all calls, though Nate didn't like it. But it might be Harper's daycare provider, so she couldn't ignore her phone. But she did look at the display.

"It's Sylvia," she said.

Nate leaned toward her. "What does she want?"

The phone rang again, and she tilted her head. "As I haven't talked to her yet, I don't know."

"Then talk to her."

She put the phone to her ear, aware of Nate's stare as she listened to Sylvia. "Yes, I'll be there," she said when Sylvia was done. "Thanks for letting me know." She hung up, setting her phone next to her tablet.

"You look pensive," Nate said. "Want to talk about it?"

"There's a town board meeting tonight. A couple deputies are going to talk about firework safety." She sucked in her breath. "Sylvia said that after they're done, August will be speaking."

"About what?"

"I don't know." A chill went through her. "He specifically asked her to tell me about it."

"He wants you there."

She nodded. "Can you babysit tonight?"

"Hell no. Ask the kid next door. Or her daytime sitter. I'm going to the meeting, too."

"You don't live here."

"I'm living here for the next two weeks. That makes me a native."

"That makes you a tourist. A nosy one."

"I'm dating a native. What does that make me?"

"A dirty old man."

He laughed. "Nosy and dirty. I like that."

"Perverted, too."

"Not perverted. And not old. If all goes well, I have a few decades left. Until then, I'm enjoying life. Besides, you could use my support."

She made a face. "Being unpopular is a character-building experience."

"Your character has strong muscles."

"When I'm snubbed or see people whispering about me, I remind myself that I took karate lessons."

"I heard about that. How many years of karate did you have?"

"Three, and I still remember a few moves." She picked up the phone as Misty strolled in, heading toward her water and food bowls in the corner. "I'll see if Katie can babysit tonight. I don't want to miss the meeting."

"I get the feeling that the place will be packed." Goose bumps rose on her arms. "And I get the feeling it's going to be a very interesting evening."

Forty-three

Twenty minutes before the meeting was going to start, Elle and Nate entered the town hall—a plain room with double rows of six folding tables and chairs facing a dais and a table where the board members sat. Elle noticed that Sylvia wasn't sitting with them. It looked like there wasn't enough room for all of the members, and Sylvia had been the loser. Or the winner.

Folding chairs lined the walls of the room, too, and about three-quarters were already filled. Heads were turned toward her and Nate, and she didn't suspect it had anything to do with Nate's pleated khaki shorts that stopped about an inch above his knees or his Hawaiian-styled shirt, red with white flowers.

No, the stares were aimed at her. If they were bullets, she would be writhing on the floor with multiple holes in her head and body.

That reminded her that it had been a long time since she'd writhed on a floor. Or a bed. She started to laugh but turned it into coughs.

"Something wrong?" Nate asked.

She shook her head, hearing the door open

behind her. She spotted two empty chairs on the left side of the wall, about nine chairs down from the dais. "This way."

As they headed to the chairs, careful not to step on anyone's feet, she got nods and bright glances of curiosity. Only three men and two women pursed their lips and looked away.

As they did, she thought, *I'll remember you.*

It wasn't that she held grudges, but she remembered idiots—and they weren't people she wanted to associate with.

She sat next to Beth, who worked at the ice cream parlor. Beth put her hand on Elle's arm and squeezed. Elle smiled at her and ordered herself not to think the squeeze of friendship had anything to do with Elle's cherry ice cream fetish—though lately she'd been switching it up with peanut butter crunch ice cream. And once in a while, she even had vanilla.

So many choices, so many calories...

More people were heading in, the bodies heating up the big room that could use more air. Elle sat forward to peer at the back, and she saw people lining up in the back, standing. Nate slanted toward her. "I hope no one stands in front of us."

As she nodded, someone harrumphed in the front. Then a screech that hurt Elle's ears came from the elderly microphone. She was still wincing when John Norman's voice came through the mic as a shout.

"Can someone close the doors? It's time to start the meeting, and we're going to get mosquitoes."

"And lower the volume," a man's voice called out from the back.

Norman glared at him as someone tried to close the door, and there was a raised voice from someone coming in. Nate took out his phone from his pocket and started tapping something in it.

"What are you doing?" Elle whispered.

"Notes for my next screenplay."

She held back a giggle. If anyone guessed what Nate was doing, she suspected they would both get kicked out.

The door was finally closed, and John Norman made a big production of introducing the deputies, one older man and one younger. The younger stood and looked tall and manly as the older deputy talked for twenty minutes, basically saying, "Don't put off any fireworks or you might lose a hand."

By the time he finished the first sentence, Nate stuck his phone back in his pocket and sat back. Elle had a hard time holding back yawns, and she looked around, noticing Janet and Lissa Norman at the front table, both of them glancing back at her, glaring.

She smiled at them. She waved. They turned to the front.

On the table next to theirs sat Duke and Pilar, their expressions serious. They had water bottles in front of them, and they were holding hands.

Elle scanned the other tables for August but didn't see him. Then she scanned the people on the left who were sitting on the folding chairs. As she did, the right side of her face tingled. She twisted to the right. And there he was, five chairs down from the front.

August. Looking straight at her.

Her breath caught.

Her heart beat harder.

August.

That's all she thought, her mind blank. Just *August.*

Why were they meeting like this? What had happened to him?

What had happened to her?

And what had happened to the happily ever after she'd been secretly hoping for? So secretly she hadn't admitted it to herself.

But she was a psychologist. She knew how wrong it was to think like that. There wasn't a happily ever after. There were only moments of happiness, and she made them with her own mind, her own choices. Laughing at Nate's witticisms. Playing with Harper. Loving Harper. Talking to her friends, her mom.

Sometimes staying all night with a friend who needed her.

No matter what the fallout, no matter if she wanted more, she was honored and grateful to have been there for August. It was a night she was not going to regret.

She must have missed John Norman's introduction of August, because he walked past her toward the dais. As he did, she held her head high.

Forty-four

On the speaker platform, August took a couple gulps of water. During the short delay, people began whispering. His throat wetted, he set the water bottle down then angled the microphone toward himself and bent down a couple inches.

He hadn't written a speech, but he remembered the important parts. "I know you," he began, his voice booming out from the microphone. He paused, and murmurs and excited whispers rose up in the room in front of him.

Pulling back from the microphone, he glanced around the room and let his eyes linger on Kevin Hunt, who'd fixed the plumbing last Tuesday in room thirty-eight, then on Sandi Morgan who waitressed at The Magic Tree. She was six months pregnant and single, and since he'd noticed her growing belly, he sometimes stopped by just to sit at a table of hers and leave a triple-sized tip.

Then his gaze settled on Grey and Minnie Underwood. Grey had macular degeneration and could barely see, but he often said he was lucky, because now Minnie was his eyes as well as his heart.

One by one, the murmurs died down.

As the silence stretched out, the tension in the room stretched, too, like a rubber band on the verge of snapping. Standing back from the microphone, he said to the room, "I know all of you."

Instead of continuing, he looked at these people he knew so well. *Really* looked at them, the way he'd looked at Kevin, Grey, and Minnie. Starting at the left, his gaze slid down the room, at the townspeople sitting by the tables and the dozen or more people standing in the back. Then his gaze slid up the room, at the townspeople sitting by the tables at the right, lighting on Elle's red hair, but he didn't linger there. This time he didn't linger anywhere. He finished the row, then turned to look behind him at the long where most of the town's board members sat.

Again, he didn't allow his gaze to linger. He turned to face the townspeople again. Let them make up their own minds who was at fault. Audiences were good at finding fault. Especially this one.

Once he finished his talk, he hoped they would make up their minds of who was *not* at fault.

"At your heart of hearts," he said, "I believe you're good people. So it makes me sad to say that there's been gossip going around that concerns me. The strange thing is that the gossip started because a friend helped me—yet no one is putting any blame on *me*. The friend who helped me is the one who's being maligned."

Stopping to take a breath, he saw a few people looking down at their laps. They reminded him of Duke's old dog who used to hang her head and look guilty when she'd eaten something she shouldn't have eaten.

He leaned down to the microphone. "The truth is, on the night everyone is talking about, I drank too much. I've been out of the service for two years now. While there, I was a witness to something that sickened me. It was the kind of thing that eats into your soul." He paused. "I never asked for help, because I kept telling myself I'd get over it. And one way that I got over it was to numb myself with alcohol."

A buzz of whispering started. While he waited for the whispering to settle, he glanced at Elle. She was watching him back. He wasn't sure if she was sending him silent support, but he wanted to believe that, so he nodded at her. *I hear you. I feel you. Thank you.*

He turned back to the others. "For the most part, I've been able to handle myself." He shook his head. "That's what I called it. *Handling myself.* I'm a Marine. We're supposed to be disciplined, and I prided myself on my control. But the night that everyone's talking about is one that I didn't handle well. I can't even tell you what set it off, because I don't remember."

Stopping abruptly, he grabbed his water bottle again and took another couple of gulps. The place was silent, no one even whispering as he set down the bottle and leaned forward.

"All I remember is that I drank too much, and then I came home. I knew enough not to be a raging drunk in public. But once I was home, I drank some more. I lost control. And sometime during my drunken self-pity party, I called Elle Styles, told her I was sick, and asked her to come and take care of me."

Pausing to take another deep breath, he looked around, and the others were staring at him. Enthralled.

No one seemed to care about his problem. His weakness.

He didn't look at the Normans. Unlike most of his other neighbors, they would immediately see his weakness.

And if they did? His tensed muscles relaxed. This wasn't about him. It wasn't about his reputation. They'd get past it. His dad and mom already knew about this. They were the ones who mattered.

And Elle... She knew about it. She mattered. And she was getting the flack for it.

Not anymore. Not if he could stop it.

"Elle held my hand, and she stayed with me. While I slept on the couch, she slept in the chair. While I was still sleeping my drinking binge off, she left in the morning, and she walked out with her head high, not trying to hide, because she'd done nothing wrong. But someone saw her."

A cry came, and he knew it was from Melanie, the desk clerk who'd started the gossip.

"I don't blame this person for passing it on. She saw something, and she talked about it. That's human nature. But somewhere along the line, the talk turned ugly. As if someone had an agenda against Elle."

Another gasp came, and then the whisperings got excited.

He let the whispers rise and then fall. Only then did he speak again.

"I have my own opinion on who's behind this maliciousness and nastiness, but I'm not pointing fingers. All I'm saying is that whatever you think Elle Styles did, you're wrong. She's been a good friend to me. And as for me, since that night, I haven't drunk anything alcoholic."

He turned to Elle, and she was smiling at him.

Were tears running down her cheeks? Happy tears, he hoped, but he was too far away to see that well.

Then she lifted her hand and brushed a knuckle along one cheekbone and then the other.

Yes, tears.

For him.

He looked down at the thin veneered wood of the dais for a moment, then he lifted his chin. From the front table, Duke gave him a thumbs up, and he nodded at Duke, ready to continue.

"Sally Hayes can attest," he said, "that I have traded in the booze for ice cream."

He waited for the burst of laughter to ebb.

"That's all I came to say. I'm not here to malign anyone's reputation. I'm just here to save one. Thank you for staying and listening to me."

As he stepped down, the clapping started.

He didn't know what he'd expected, but not this.

He ducked his head, then walked to the left, on the side opposite of where Elle was sitting, and no one left as they usually did. He didn't know why.

But as he walked down the aisle, he shook hands, and he thanked the people individually. There must've been more than a good hundred. Standing room only. Probably the maximum, and some people had been turned away.

It almost felt like he was someone special, instead of just one of them. A man who'd screwed up and now everyone knew about it.

He reached Chuck, who was sitting with his mother—probably dragged there by Sylvia, Chuck got up, then pounded his back.

Sylvia stood, too, and she, who'd always been so dignified and reserved, hugged him then stepped back. "You're a good man."

As he looked into her cool blue eyes that were a little teary, he felt as if he had been given a benediction. He wanted to tell her that she was looking at the wrong person. He wasn't a hero. Nowhere near one. He was flawed.

But she was smart enough to know that already, so he thanked her, then moved on. He kept shaking hands, looking straight into faces. Straight into eyes. Young and middle-aged and old. The age he'd been, the age he was now, and the ages he would be. Because of Elle's big heart, they were all faces he knew. Something he'd planned to mention, but he'd forgotten.

Too late now. But they knew who he was. And they knew where he came from and how he'd gotten here.

He reached the door, and the whole time he'd circled the place, he'd avoided looking at the tables, because he knew who was sitting there.

So he looked at the tables now, and half of

them were turned to look at him. But that one table in front, the place where John, Janet, and Lissa Norman were sitting, all had their backs to him.

And on the other side, he could see that not everyone had waited for him to come around. That some of the people had left.

One of them was Elle.

He thanked everyone for coming, then he walked out the door.

He had someplace else to go and someone else he needed to talk to.

Forty-five

The knock on the front door startled Elle. Misty meowed sharply, jumped off her lap, and ran into the hall. Nate had stayed back with Sylvia. Though they were unlike any couple she knew, she was glad they were finding some romance.

She wouldn't mind finding some herself, but it didn't look like that was going to happen. Not here, anyway.

She took her time heading to the door. It was dark out already. Newly dark, where the sky was charcoal-gray, and she could still see the paler gray clouds in the sky and the slice of the moon out of the front window, the gray-and-white view looking like a comic strip frame.

There was no peephole, so she opened the door a crack—and there he was. August. Standing on the stoop. Looking at her.

She opened the door the rest of the way. "Are you parked out front?" she asked, her voice low.

"Yes." One side of his mouth quirked up; the other side remained straight.

The two sides of August. And she couldn't read either one. "Idiot. Park in back."

His gaze on her remained as steady as a one-hundred-pound rock. "I'm not hiding."

She glared at him, and the other side of his lips quirked up to match the right side. As if this were one big joke.

"Idiot," she said again, then stepped back to let him in. "You just convinced them I was the next Mother Teresa. I had to flee before they converged on me and begged me to pray for them."

Stepping inside, he laughed low in his throat, giving her shivers.

"What are you doing here?" she demanded.

"Giving up. I can't resist you."

She crossed her arms. "You are starting to piss me off."

"I don't want to piss you off. I want to love you."

"Oh, you do?" She tapped her bare foot on the worn gray carpet. And she couldn't help but notice that with his shoes on and hers off, she was even shorter than usual compared to him.

She really hated that.

"You're in a bad mood," he said. "Something I did?"

She let out a long breath, and the tightness in her shoulders relaxed. She peered up at him. "I didn't think coming here for six weeks would be so stressful."

"My fault," he said.

"My emotions aren't your fault."

"I have nothing to do with your emotions?"

She closed her eyes, then felt herself sway. Though he didn't move closer, remaining a couple feet away, his hand wrapped around her arm, and her eyes snapped open.

"What are you doing?" she asked.

"Keeping you from falling."

"I fall every time I see you." She closed her eyes again, but even in the nighttime, he was like a shining sun, too bright for her to stare at. She opened them again. He was so beautiful. Too beautiful. "You need to stop playing with me."

"I've wanted to make love to you for years." His voice was rough.

"You turned me down."

"I was...afraid."

"Of what?" she whispered, not taking her eyes off his face.

"That you wouldn't stay. That you would go away again."

"I was thinking of staying here, and then..." She shrugged. "Well, you know what happened."

"Me," he said. "I happened."

She stared at him. "Don't you know, August? You happened to me a long ago. Since I was a child, I felt like I shared a bond with you."

"We grew up. I was here, and you weren't."

"You weren't by me, either. Our paths were different."

"Life kept us apart." His voice was husky. "Maybe it's time we took control of our lives."

She swallowed. "What do you suggest we do? Sex?"

"It's not all about sex."

"I agree. Not everything is about sex. But what about tonight?" Keeping that thought in her mind, she smiled slowly, then she jutted her hip out.

His eyes darkened.

Good. Very good.

"Now that people won't treat me like the whore of Babylon..." She made her voice low and breathy—she was a psychologist, and she knew the ways that turned on a man, and it was about damn time she used that knowledge. "I might consider it again."

He smiled slowly. "Yeah?"

"*If* you convince me to let you stay."

His smile widened, then he took a step toward her. At the same time, she stepped toward him, and their bodies bumped together. She jumped back, and he stepped back. She raised her head to laugh, but he wasn't laughing back. The intense look on his face, his eyes burning into hers, stopped her laughter. Taking her into his arms, he leaned down, pulled her against him, and kissed her.

She held on to him tightly. She was melting. Melting fast. Like butter on a Trouble Bay sidewalk in June. Melting right into his arms.

When the kiss finished, she made a noise that sounded a lot like a purr to her. And she'd listened to a lot of cats purring.

"Can we go to your bedroom?" he asked.

"We can and we may." She smiled. "But we can't be too loud. I don't want to wake Harper." Or disturb Misty, who was probably hiding in Nate's room.

"Neither do I," he said. "What about your writing partner?"

"He didn't give me his itinerary, but he's not here. I think he has his eyes on Sylvia."

"Sylvia?" His eyebrows shot up. "I can't picture them together. Like the princess and the clown."

She took his hand. "I see Sylvia as more of a queen." She stepped back, pulling him with her. "And I think both queens and princesses like to laugh."

"What about you?"

"I've been wanting you for so long." She could hear her voice getting throaty, on the edge of tears. "If we don't do something soon, it will be no laughing matter."

He made a growling sound, like a hungry animal, and she laughed breathlessly. If he was growling, that must make her his meal...and strangely, she didn't mind one bit the thought of being eaten by him.

Forty-six

August picked her up in his arms. She laughed again. "Put me down. I don't want you to strain yourself before we make love."

"You mean *after* we make love it's okay if I hurt myself?" He smiled down at her, and he wasn't a smiley kind of guy. Not since he'd returned from his last tour. But it only took one look at her in his arms for him to smile. For him to feel good. For him to feel that life wasn't just work and play and one day after another going by, with the seasons changing and the guests at the hotel changing.

It was a good life, but something had been missing. Missing for too long.

And now, holding her in his arms, *nothing* was missing. The click that happened when one part fit into another...that's how he felt. They fit together. They were two halves that made a whole.

"Yes." She grinned at him, her eyes sparkling like sunlight on water. "After you make love to me, you can injure yourself. I'm selfish and only care about my pleasure."

"What about the pleasure I plan on having?"

"What pleasure? I'm just going to lie there and let you lick me and suck me and caress me all over."

"All over your body?"

She laughed. "I don't want you to miss a spot."

"Sounds like it will take awhile."

"A *very* long while."

Happiness rose up inside him. "What happens when I'm done?"

Her eyebrows arched. "Do you need me to explain what happens then?"

"I think I can figure out the logistics." Laughter was inside him. Joy. He was smiling at her and couldn't seem to stop.

"In that case, you'd better get going, soldier."

"Marine," he said, and as he said it, he didn't feel fractured or guilty or depressed. Instead, he felt proud. He and the men and women he knew had joined the Marines to help their country and help people in other countries, too. No matter what happened or what didn't happen, their intentions were always the best.

She'd saved him as a child, and she was healing him as an adult. It wasn't what she said, it was *who* she was—an amazing woman with happiness beaming out of her pores.

As he carried her to the bedroom, peace settled inside him.

Maybe he would decide later that he needed to talk to her about the depression he'd been feeling for so long. But right now—right this minute, this second, this instant of time, he only felt wonderful. And lucky. And everything good.

And he had the feeling that in the next half hour—and maybe for hours longer—it was going to get even more amazing.

Forty-seven

As August carried her to the end of the hallway, she whispered to him that her bedroom was next to Harper's. He nodded, understanding that he needed to be quiet.

Inside the bedroom, she wiggled out of his grasp. He let her go, holding her until her feet slipped to the floor, then he turned to close the door. When he turned back, she was pulling off her top.

"Great idea," he said, his voice low.

"What?"

"To get rid of these clothes."

She giggled and he grinned. It felt like the happiness was bursting out of him.

She finished first, her clothes on the floor. He put his on the small chair by the bureau, and he was grinning wider, because now he knew that she was messier than him. She sure as hell couldn't be more eager.

And then she jumped up at him, and he caught her. It felt as if he were young again. As if all the bad things that had happened were washed away for this moment. Holding her, the wonder, the joy, the emotion built up inside him. And along with that was *need* and *want*. So powerful and wonderful.

Overwhelming him when he wanted to treasure this moment.

He fell onto the bed with his arms wrapped tightly around her.

"I never want to let you go."

"I know." She had to crane back her head. Her eyes gazed into his, and in the blueness, he saw the dark glow. The fire. Her skin was smooth and warm, and it felt good against him. His body agreed.

For some reason he couldn't understand, this woman, this amazing woman, wanted him.

"I wanted you all along," he said, "but because of you, I'd already been given so much. I didn't feel I deserved more. I didn't feel I deserved *you.*"

"Don't you know how incredible you are?" she asked. "How wonderful?"

"No."

She smiled at him then. Slowly. "Later, I can tell you with words. Now, I think it's time to tell you with actions. We've waited so long. And I want you now. More than anything, I want you."

He shifted so he was on top of her. "I'm going to love you," he said, and heard the thickness of his voice, "like you've never been loved before."

Her eyes lit up. "A lot of talk. But so far no action."

He rolled her over so she was on her back on the bed, and he was on top of her. "It's time for me to fix that, isn't it?"

"Exactly what I've been trying to tell you."

She laughed again, and he closed his eyes as he kissed her, and he just *felt* how well they fit together, despite their height differences. As if she were made for him. And he was made for her.

Her laughter slowed, becoming breathy, and he angled his head to kiss the soft spot under her jaw. Her breath sucked in.

And then it got even better...

Forty-eight

August was kissing and touching her in places that hadn't been kissed and touched in too long, and she was on fire. Burning. Squirming.

"I'm ready for this." She clutched his shoulders so tightly that she thought her nails would leave imprints. "Don't wait. I'm feeling crazy hot now. Make love to me *now*. Any more and it's not lovemaking, it's torture."

His dark eyes stared into hers, and it seemed to her that he was on fire, too. "Condom," he said, and rolled away.

She closed her eyes and just breathed. She'd waited a long time for this, and now here they were. Finally together.

And then he was back, on top of her, his skin warm, his lips on top of hers. "I think I'm in love with you," he whispered.

She closed her eyes.

"I want to worship you."

Her eyelids snapped up. "I am a goddess," she said.

He laughed, and she saw the exultation in his face. And it made her feel good.

Then his hand moved down between them, and he touched her. Her breath sucked in, and she had to stop herself from shouting, making only a mewling sound. As she held onto his shoulders, he said in the same gravelly voice, "I want to worship you."

She put her hand over his arm and sucked in a breath. It was good, so good.

But she knew what would be even better.

"Worship later," she said. "Come inside me now. I don't want to wait any longer."

He pulled his hand away, then fitted himself against her, on top of her, his skin warm, his lips on top of hers, fitting himself against her, fitting himself against her. She felt so tight, and he felt so good, going in slow. Very slow.

She gripped his shoulders tightly. He made a sound of satisfaction, and she wrapped her legs around him. Then he groaned, and she opened her eyes wide and looked at his face with the flushed cheeks and the half-lidded eyes.

He looked like a man under a spell.

Good. Because she was a woman under *his* spell.

"I wanted to go slower," he muttered.

"If you go any slower, I'd have to kill you."

"You say the sweetest things," he said, and was laughing as he moved faster.

She arched her back, and she sucked in the urge to shout out his name. To scream it. To yell out how good it felt. How right.

She wrapped her legs more tightly around his thighs as he moved, and he moved, and he moved.

And she moved back, feeling the slide of him touching all the right spots that drove her crazy. The spots that made her pulse around him and moan.

"It's good," she whispered as she arched her back. "It's good, it's good, it's good, it's good."

Then her words stopped, and so did her thoughts as her body convulsed around him, and she just *felt*. Gripping him tightly. Whimpering. Not wanting to let him go.

And then he was still, pulsing inside her. And her body went limp.

And finally when it was over, she was spent and feeling delicious, almost the way she did after a wonderful meal only there was no stuffed-belly syndrome. Just nirvana. Just bliss and fulfillment and loved. Thoroughly loved.

This wasn't just sex. This was happiness.

She closed her eyes, and she felt herself going to sleep, August heavy on top of her.

Forty-nine

As usual, Sylvia woke up early. Through the cracks of the curtains, dim early-morning light entered the room.

As usual.

What wasn't usual was the heavy breathing next to her.

Keeping her eyes closed, she relished the sound. Relished the warmth coming from the sleeping body next to her. Not touching, but so close she could smell him.

The smell was good. The smell of a man. The smell of last night's sex.

The way her body felt...stretched and treasured and *used*...was even better.

She lay there, the corners of her lips curved, enjoying the moment. Feeling good. Very, very, *very* good. Finally, she inhaled deeply, holding that feeling inside her until she had to exhale. Then she rolled to her side and carefully slid out of bed so as not to make the mattress bounce. Not wanting to awaken him until he was ready to awaken.

She was careful closing the connected bathroom door, too. She showered quickly, then put on her rose-colored cotton robe. When she came back into the bedroom, she left the light on in the bathroom, the door slightly ajar, so she didn't have to turn on the bedroom light. Nate still slept, making woofing noises on his exhales, like a dog her parents had when she was younger who used to whiffle in his sleep. She found her underwear, her gray-green capris, and a top. She almost forgot her bra but remembered at the last minute, then went back into the bathroom to change.

When she returned to the bedroom, the light peeking in was brighter, and she turned off the bathroom light. Nate was snoring softly now, on his side, his gray hair unruly and his nose prominent even in sleep.

Well, why not? It didn't naturally get smaller. Not like his penis. The thought made her want to giggle like a teenage girl, and she held the laughter back, still looking at him, though he wasn't a man of beauty.

She didn't care. Charley had been a man of beauty on the outside but ugly on the inside.

She was ninety-nine percent sure that with Nate, it was the opposite. She was a much better judge now than when she was young.

For once, she wanted to stay in bed. Stay with *him*. But with a sigh, she stepped away, closed the door softly, and headed to the kitchen.

Life went on.

When she was a young woman, a few of her local friends had had a summer fling with tourists. Nate was her first summer fling. She quite liked it.

Heading down the hallway, she hummed. Not any particular song, just humming tunelessly.

Before anything else, she started the coffee and the tea in the dining room. Her breakfast was slated to start at eight a.m., but if someone woke earlier, they could at least have coffee and tea.

Then she headed to the kitchen to start the big breakfast. She took out of the pantry the ingredients for her lemon-blueberry muffins and started measuring. All five of her guestrooms were filled, and her muffins were always a hit. If the weather continued, she would break even this year. She frowned, because she was still paying on her loan for the renovations.

It hadn't been an easy year for her.

Damn insurance.

She knew that what she'd done to her insurance agent was wrong...but she couldn't regret it.

Thoughts about the shooting stopped her humming. She got eggs from her fridge and, in a small bowl, mixed them with milk, melted butter, and vanilla, then poured the mixture into the dry ingredients and stirred with the wooden spoon that had belonged to her mother. Then she spooned it into the muffin tins and put them in the preheated oven.

The work soothed her. Allowed her to breathe easier.

She didn't stop there. She put fruit out. The abundance of fruit made summer her favorite time of year. And then she started the French toast. She planned on making scrambled eggs, too, but they weren't as popular as her French toast or her muffins. The only complaints she got about either of those were that they ate too much of them.

She loved those kinds of complaints.

The door opened from the hall as she whisked together the cinnamon, nutmeg, and sugar. She turned and looked at Nate, feeling suddenly shy.

"Hello, beautiful," he said.

She laughed breathlessly.

He stepped inside, the door swinging shut behind him. "Are you embarrassed?"

"I told you last night," she said, feeling her cheeks warm, "that I don't do this often."

He stepped up to the table. "Explain often."

She pressed her lips together and shook her head. "I know you're a professor, so I'll just say that this is a test I won't pass."

His smile slid, and he just looked at her with his brown eyes that were the most beautiful thing about him. "There's no test. I'm a lucky man. May I take you out for dinner tonight?"

"You may."

He bent toward her, and she leaned toward him, and they kissed a little awkwardly. He backed away, slowly, as if he didn't want to leave.

She liked his awkwardness. He seemed so confident, but she liked the way he wasn't quite sure of her.

"I'll see you at six?" he said.

She nodded, her mind already going to what she should wear. He smiled, looking younger—but still not handsome.

And it didn't matter. He made her feel beautiful. He made her feel sexy. He made her feel like a woman who'd had great sex last night.

A woman who might get lucky again later this night.

He left then, and she hummed again, picking up the whisk. The land phone rang, and she looked over at it, holding the whisk, not wanting to talk to anyone who might ruin her mood. But it rang again, and she put down the whisk. It could be someone who wanted to reserve a room.

She wiped her hands on her apron. On the display area, she saw Sheldon's name, her cousin. She sighed though she liked her cousin. He made her laugh, and he was good at computers and had fixed hers. So of course, she had to pick it up, even if his timing wasn't convenient.

"Hi, Sheldon. I'm making breakfast now—"

"I need to see you."

"Um..."

"You can't tell anyone about this. No one."

"Sheldon, are you all right?"

He laughed harshly, and Sheldon was not a man who laughed harshly. Sheldon was a man who loved his dogs, who loved the hats in his Trouble Bay Hat Trick Shoppe, and who loved his partner, who spoke with a lovely Irish accent.

"What's wrong?" she asked, hearing the high note in her voice.

"I'll tell you when I see you. Just know that we've been screwed."

She frowned and agreed to meet him at ten that morning.

Then he hung up, and she put down the phone slowly.

As she did, she thought she'd been screwed last night, but that had been a good screwing.

She suspected the screwing Sheldon wanted to share with her wasn't pleasant at all.

Fifty

August was smiling, and he couldn't remember the last morning he'd woken up feeling good. But he had never woken up next to Elle.

A noise came from the room next to him, startling him. A girl's voice sang out. Something about a bird, and next he heard a thump—feet jumping on the floor. Then running feet headed into the bathroom door across the hall, the door shutting.

Next to him, Elle turned over and looked at him with her eyes opened wide. Before he could say anything, the front door opened and then closed. And a man's voice sang, "When a Man Loves a Woman" out of key.

A cat meowed, clearly objecting to the off-tune singing.

Elle put her hand over her mouth and giggled.

August turned to Elle and kissed her.

She kissed him back. "You know what we have here?"

"Life," he said.

She laughed and nodded.

"And love," he added.

Her laughter stopped, and her lips parted.

Before she could say anything, the bedroom door pushed open, and Harper skipped into the room, wearing a pink pajama set with gray kittens, her curly hair messy. Seeing him, she stopped halfway to the bed.

"Mommy, what's Uncle August doing in your bed?"

He swallowed a groan and ignored his instinct to pull the blanket over his head. At least the blanket covered most of his body.

Elle pulled her blanket up to her shoulders. "Sweetheart, we were having a sleepover."

"Girls don't have sleepovers with boys," Harper said, her voice ringing with authority.

"Honey—"

"Let me handle it." August wondered why the hell he hadn't rushed to get clothes on when he'd heard Harper waking up. He just hadn't thought that she'd rush into the room without knocking. This was a new situation for him.

"There's nothing for you to handle," Elle said.

"That's not what I meant. I meant—" He stopped, smart enough to know that anything he said to defend himself would be a mistake.

The only thing he could do to make it better was to man up. He turned back to Harper and took a deep breath.

"Harper, it's okay to sleep with your mommy if she's going to marry me."

"You're marrying my mommy?"

"No!" Elle said.

"I am," he said, "but only if your mom says yes."

"Mommy!" Harper jumped up and down. "Please say you'll marry him. He can be my live-in daddy. We can live by Uncle Duke and Aunt Pilar."

"Harper, honey—"

Harper jumped up and down. "And I can have a puppy!"

"Honey!"

"Yes," he said. "You can have a puppy."

Elle socked his arm muscle. Hard.

Harper gasped. "Mom, you hit him!" Then she fell onto the bedroom rug, giggling.

Elle scowled at him. "I'm so mad at you."

"And I'm so in love with you," he said. "And I have been since I was eight years old."

"Oh, you..." Her eyes moistened, and he bent and kissed her.

Fifty-one

August walked away from his parked car to his chalet, a spring in his step. The morning sun was bright, and so was his day. As bright as his night with her had been.

Everything felt bright right now. His whole future.

Elle hadn't said yes.

But she hadn't said no.

He used his key to unlock the door, and he stepped in, tossing the jacket he hadn't worn on the chair, heading to the bedroom to take off his clothes and leave them on the floor before he went to the bathroom for a shower.

As he strode into his bedroom, he saw a woman in his bed. Lissa. Pushing up from the pillow, her shoulders bare, his light blue blanket covering the rest of her. Her eyes were blinking as if she'd just woken.

He halted. He vaguely recalled giving her a key once, though he couldn't remember why.

She must have had another key made.

"What are you doing here?" he demanded, but was drowned out by the angry tone of her voice.

"Where the fuck were you?" She pushed off the bed, standing at the side, not covering up her nakedness. Her long, too-slender body tilted forward, her face forward even more, looming at him.

"Lissa—"

"No! I'm not listening to any excuses." Her face was turning red. "I came here last night so you could apologize. But you weren't here. I waited for you, and you never came. You were with *her*, weren't you?"

"Get dressed." He spoke low, standing with his feet apart, his body braced for trouble. "I don't know what's wrong with you, but you're way out of line."

"I'll tell you what's wrong with me. I'm angry as hell."

"You're crazy as hell. I'll give you five minutes to get out, or I'm calling the sheriff." He pulled his phone out of his pocket.

Her body straightened. Her head jerked back. "You can't do that to me."

"The hell I can't."

"We were *lovers*."

He winced. Shit. She'd chased after him, not the other way around. She was convenient, but she'd never meant anything to him. And he was sure she'd never meant anything to her, either. Sure that the only person she really cared about was herself.

But he couldn't throw that in her face. Her selfishness had suited him. It had enabled him to use her and not care that he didn't respect or even like her.

Though now he saw he'd only been able to do that because he'd been in a place where he hadn't respected and loved himself.

"Look, Lissa, we had fun, but I never made any promises. It's not like you cared for me."

"You're wrong." Her head tilted in an odd way. With her unblinking stare and thin body, it made her look a little creepy. "I cared for you from the moment I saw you."

"If my father hadn't adopted me, you wouldn't have given me a second look." He narrowed his eyes. "How many men of Mexican descent besides me have you dated?"

"If not for your adopted father, do you think Elle Styles would have dated you?" Her mouth twisted into a snarl. "That's who you were with last night, isn't it?"

"I mean it. I'm calling the sheriff."

She made a dismissive movement with her hand. "Elle has a child! And there's no husband in sight. The child's father must have realized that she's a whore."

"That's it." He turned on his phone.

"You call the sheriff, and I'll kill her."

Still holding the phone, he went still. "I'll be sure to tell the sheriff about your threat."

"I don't even have to be there. I can pay someone to kill her."

"You can't make me love you by threatening me."

She drew in a breath, her breasts expanding, and then the breath shuddered out, her eyes still staring crazily at him.

"I'll get dressed," she said, her voice low. "And

I'll leave. But *you* are mine. If I see you with her, I don't know what I'll do."

In silence, he watched her get dressed, which she did quickly, her eyes only leaving his as she pulled her top back on, her white shorts, and her high-heeled sandals.

She strode up to him, stopping inches away as he watched her grimly.

"Remember what I said." Her voice was hard, her mouth angry. "I see you with her, and she's a dead woman."

Then she strutted away, her hips swaying and her steps strong, as if she were a model on a runway instead of a crazy ex-girlfriend who was vibrating with hatred.

As he watched her leave, he felt cold.

She would do it. She would kill Elle. Or at the least, try to kill her.

No one else had heard her threats. The deputies might believe him, but they wouldn't do anything. After all, look who her father was.

His front door closed, and he stepped to it, double locking the door. He needed to go to the hardware store to get new locks for his doors.

He plopped down on a chair, his eyes closed, his mind working.

Elle had rented the cottage for only six weeks. It was nearly five weeks now. When the six weeks were over, he would follow Elle to Madison, and he would propose to her. This time he'd do it the right way. On bended knee, and a ring in his pocket. Maybe something for Harper, too. A puppy. She would like that. They would marry in Madison. Or maybe in Green Bay.

He would tell Duke about Lissa's threats. Duike could talk to her father.

His thoughts eased the tension that tightened the muscles in his neck and back. He breathed easier.

If Elle called him, he would tell her about Lissa's threats, and his solution. Otherwise it would be best to stay away from her until he could hook up with her in Madison.

Lissa didn't love him. He didn't believe that for a moment. What he did believe was that she thought whatever she wanted, she would get. And she wanted him because she knew he would someday inherit the resort. She didn't give a damn about him. And he sure the hell didn't owe her anything.

In three days there would be the fireworks.

And two weeks after that, Elle would be gone.

And so would he be gone. Chasing after her. And this time he wasn't coming back without her and Harper, and a wedding ring on her left hand.

Fifty-two

Sylvia's mind was numb. Sitting in Sheldon's small office in the back of the hat shop he co-owned with his life and work partner, Adrian, she sipped the organic green tea he'd said would be good for her.

Right now, the only thing good for her would be a glass of hard whiskey.

She looked down at the marbled paper-covered journals on his classic cherry desk. The desk was old but in perfect condition, unlike the journals which had worn spots in places where thumbs and fingers had held them through the many years.

"I don't think I heard right." Sylvia heard her voice, but something was wrong with her ears, because it felt as if her words came from far away. As if someone else were saying it.

Her life had just turned upside down.

Again.

The first time it had happened, she'd found out her husband was a liar, a cheat—and stupid, too.

Too stupid to be afraid when she'd pointed the gun at him. Never believing she would shoot him.

The second time had been when she'd realized her insurance agent was cheating her so he didn't have to report that he'd forgotten to send her check in. And—bonus for him—his insurance company wouldn't have to pay to repair her house.

She suspected that, in the last seconds of his life, he'd regretted that decision.

But now she was finding out that her family had been duped since 1880. And she'd been made a fool, too, by the same family.

"You're sure it's real?" The pitiful wobble in her voice made her wince.

A spear of sunlight shooting through the window illuminated the diary, and she thought it was a sign from God. Or maybe from some of her dead relatives, telling her to snap out of it and smell the treachery.

"It's real, all right," Sheldon said. "The short explanation is that I joined an online ancestry loop, and another ancestry researcher in Connecticut knew someone who had a great-great relative from Trouble Bay in Wisconsin."

"Hard to forget the name of our town," she said.

"It got its name because there was a lot of trouble in the beginning, and now we know why." His eyes narrowed. "And now we know who."

She nodded. Unlike Sheldon, she'd never been interested in her ancestry. When the past was done, she was done with it.

Until the ugliness and treachery slapped her in her face, and she couldn't pretend it hadn't happened.

"She sent you the diary?" Sylvia reached out to touch the top journal but, at the last moment, pulled her hand back.

"Elizabeth said no one else in the family is interested. She's in her eighties, and she's had a couple of strokes. She suspects that when she dies, her family will throw the diaries in the trash. She only sent me the first diary that mentions what Josephine's father did. The other diaries are about Josephine's life in Connecticut with her new husband and children, and she's giving them to a Connecticut historical society."

She looked up at his handsome face, with the still-firm jaw and no sagging beneath his chin, though he was nearing sixty. He still had his hair, too. It was the same color brown as when he was a teen, and she strongly suspected he dyed it.

It was too bad that his genes wouldn't be passed on to another generation, but that was life. And if anyone knew that good looks didn't mean life would be better, it was certainly her.

And from what she'd seen, her ancestors had been handsome, too. So very likely, being cheated and lied to also ran in the family.

"You want to read it?" He pushed the diary closer to her. "Turn to page ten."

She peered down at the inoffensive diary and the faded ink, with the handwriting so beautiful it looked like calligraphy. Her eyes damp with tears, she shook her head. Though she considered herself a tough woman, she was still surprised by the treachery of man.

"Maybe later. I might start dripping tears on the pages. Tell me again what Josephine said."

"Okay." He sighed. "Hawthorne Blakeslee, the son of our first ancestors who lived in Trouble Bay—"

"I know that much."

"There's more that we never knew. The family business was ship building, but Hawthorne's dad, Edmund, had a lot of land, and he had planted cedar trees as a backup, in case things didn't go well. And they didn't. They'd been having a few bad years. His father had died suddenly. So he and his mother decided to build a sawmill and cut down the trees. They didn't have enough money for the sawmill, so they borrowed it from their neighbor."

"John Norman's ancestor." Sylvia heard the dullness of her voice. "The lucky Normans."

"I guess the Normans heard the old adage that if you want luck, you need to make your own luck."

"By stealing ours."

"Apparently, because one hot August night when it hadn't rained for a long time, there was a fire that burned the cedars and the sawmill. The family escaped, but the mother died two months later of lung congestion that was attributed to the fire. And our ancestors couldn't pay the Normans the money they'd borrowed, so they forfeited the land."

"What are you saying?"

"Not me. Josephine. She wrote that she overheard her father and older brother talking about the fire. Laughing about it."

"Did they say that they caused the fire?"

"That's what Josephine wrote."

She looked down at the journal, breathing hard, then lifted her head. "It makes me wonder about the fire that burned down my third floor. John wanted to buy it from me. Now I wonder if it was the lightning...or if it was John Norman." And had she killed the insurance agent wrongly? She swallowed. Oh, no. Oh, God, no.

"Wasn't your insurance agent a cousin of Janet Norman's?"

She stared at Sheldon. It had been so long ago that she'd forgotten, but now it came back to her.

"Yes." So the insurance company wasn't at fault, either. So it was John and her agent—and maybe Janet. Sylvia wouldn't put it past her to be part of it.

When she'd refused to sell it to John, he'd looked furious, his face red. He had even told her she was a fool for not selling it to him.

And he was right. She'd been a fool for not seeing through him. A stupid, stupid fool.

"Sylvia? Are you all right?" Sheldon's tone was concerned.

She shuddered but shook her head. "I'm fine. I wouldn't be surprised if there were some other suspicious fires that helped to enrich the Norman clan." Her fingers curled at her sides. "I'm going to kill him."

"Stand in line with wanting to kill him," Sheldon said, but he shrugged. "It's too bad we can't sue. The statute of limitations must be up."

"And we can't prove anything." Not even her house. The fire inspector had said the wiring was old, and they'd chalked it up as an electrical fire, even though her wiring had passed an inspection a few years before it had happened.

Was he in on it, too?

She stood up slowly, like an old woman. Never mind the fire inspector. She couldn't kill everyone.

But she could kill one person. "I think the lucky Normans are going to be unlucky."

He shrugged. "Their luck could be running out. Last night it was obvious that August isn't marrying their precious daughter. Someone should warn Duke and August."

"You can warn them." She turned to leave.

"Take the journal with you," he said. "In case you want to read it."

"Later. I've got an important place to go to."

"Where's that?" he asked.

Walking away, she stopped to say, "The shooting range." Then she opened the door and stepped out, thinking about Rule Number Two: *Don't let anyone cheat you.*

Which was followed by Rule Number Three: *Don't kill anyone unnecessarily.*

Her former husband: Check.

Her former insurance agent: Check.

John Norman: Almost check.

Fifty-three

"Are you marrying the boy?" Nate asked outside the open door of the bathroom.

Inside the bathroom, Elle ignored the question and tied a blue bow on one of Harper's pigtails, then tied a red ribbon on the other pigtail.

She picked Harper up so she could see herself in the mirror over the counter. Harper clapped her hands. "I'm red and blue!" she said.

"Red, white, and blue." Elle set her down.

Harper stuck up one of her legs toward Nate, showing him her white tennis shoes. "I'm the Fourth of July!"

"The princess," he said. "But is your mom kissing the frog?"

Elle glared at him. Harper giggled. "Mommy kissed August."

"Really?"

Elle closed her eyes. She wasn't going to kill him, but she might hurt him badly.

"Thank you for corrupting my daughter," she said, opening her eyes.

"Hey, I wasn't the one caught in a sleepover by your daughter. So, what are you going to do?"

"When I decide, believe me, you *won't* be the first to know."

"August wants to marry Mommy," Harper said. "He said so."

Nate bent slightly. "And what do you want, Harper?"

Her face turned serious, and Elle ached, already knowing her answer. "I want to marry him, too," Harper said. "Then we'll get to stay here forever, and I'll get to have a dog and a kitty. And I'll have a daddy."

Elle blinked away a hot rush of tears. Harper had a biological father, but his once-a-year visit didn't make a loving father.

"Sorry," Nate muttered. "I shouldn't have asked."

"No, you shouldn't have." Elle raised her eyebrows. "After all, I haven't asked you what you've been up to lately."

He frowned. "Not up to enough. Something has changed."

She winced at the melancholy on his face. "Hey." She put her hand on his arm. "We're two of a kind right now."

He patted the top of her head, like an uncle. "I think you have a better chance of a happy ever after than I do."

She shook her head as Harper said she was going to look at herself in the big mirror. Harper ran into Elle's bedroom to open the closet door and admire herself in the full-length mirror on the inside of the door.

"August feels that he owes me," Elle said, her voice low. "I'm not marrying a man because he's grateful for something I did when I was a child."

"When he looks at you, it's not gratitude I see in his face."

Her breath sucked in. She wanted to say, *Really?* But she shook her head. "I'm not convinced. If he wants me, he has to convince me. All he's done since our night together is leave a message to watch out for Lissa." She rolled her eyes. "I wonder if he'll avoid me today. Maybe I'll avoid him."

"The Fourth of July already," Nate said. "Time for fireworks. What else?"

"A parade and speeches." She grimaced. "Lissa's father will be speaking tonight at the visitors' center next to the volunteer fire department. A stage by the visitors' center was set up yesterday."

"You know all of that?"

"And more. Harper's daycare provider's husband is in the volunteer fire department. This is a big thing for the town. When I was a kid, Lissa's father was already town board chairman, and I remember he used to get up on the stage and welcome everyone before he had to get off so the bands could play. My mother used to snicker at him."

Nate smiled. "Your mother doesn't admire pomposity."

"No, she never did."

"So that's what the townspeople meant."

She raised her eyebrows in a question.

"I've heard a few women wondering aloud if John Norman was going to make any rebuttal about August's comments at the bandstand. I didn't know what they were talking about, but that must be it. I'd be more concerned about him than his daughter."

She made a face. "How is it that you've only been here a few weeks and already you know everything?"

"Not everything." Sadness shadowed his eyes again, though his mouth curved in a tight smile. "I guess I have that kind of face people trust. I think I remind them of the dead comics who used to be on TV. The sad-faced ones."

She laughed, but it was a harsh sound. "At least we'll see fireworks tonight."

He put his arm over her shoulder. "Let's go then. I'm ready for ice cream and fun."

She drew away from him to grab her purse and call her daughter. Then she looked at Nate. "I have a bad feeling about today. A really, really bad feeling."

Fifty-four

Sylvia fed her guests, then watched them leave with laughter and smiles, ready to enjoy the day. July Fourth was one of Trouble Bay's biggest holidays. Every rental unit was filled, from cottages to resorts, and so were the stores, including the art galleries, winery, pubs, restaurants, and just about every kind *of* shop there was that could be found. If people would pay good money for it, the town of Trouble Bay was likely to have it.

The townspeople were working hard to keep up with the demand. Some of the teens would be grumpy—until later this evening, when they would have money in their wallets—but the adults were smiling, because another name for the Fourth of July could be Money Day.

Money was raining down on them, and they grabbed it while it was pouring...because it didn't last. Her family knew that. Long before Door County had become a vacation mecca, they'd known it.

What they hadn't known was that they'd been cheated.

Now she knew. Her steps heavy, she headed to

her room. From her bureau, she took out the short brown wig that she'd bought at the shop in Green Bay. Amazing the difference a wig could make. The short style made her face look longer, and the dark color wasn't as flattering to her complexion as her natural blond—though the blond had needed a little unnatural help.

Her wig on, she unlocked the closet where she kept her personal and money records. Her bank key for her safety deposit box. It was also where she kept her guns.

She took out the last one, her Remington, and held it in her hands for a long time.

She couldn't use the one she had used on Charley.

The insurance agent's body hadn't surfaced, but she couldn't assume it would never be found. If she used the same gun to kill John Norman and forensics matched the guns, the sheriff's office might realize there was a connection and that it led to her.

No, she would have to use her Remington.

She sighed. It was just a gun, after all. Though money was tight, she could buy a new one.

She brought out the bullets and started to load it.

She wasn't sure when she would use it, but today, with the sun shining and so many people roaming around the town, she would look for an opening. An opportunity.

If one were determined enough, there would always be an opportunity.

John was going to be speaking today. He would go to the park this afternoon before the fireworks started. He would speak on the podium, as if everything in Trouble Bay were wonderful, and he would insinuate that he was a big reason for the success.

When in truth, he was a crook. A villain. A man who broke families.

He didn't know that she knew the truth.

And neither did he know that today—or another day very, very soon—he would die.

Fifty-five

"Hey! Boss dude." Chuck punched August's shoulder, grinning. The late-afternoon sun that was heating up the day also picked up sparks in Chuck's blue eyes, and two teen girls and their mothers strolling toward them slowed to check out Chuck.

August held back a laugh. Chuck might look like a cross between the homecoming king and Prince Charming, but he would never be the richest or the most ambitious guy in town. Still, he was easygoing, honest, and good-natured, all character traits that August admired. So he slugged Chuck in his arm back.

"What are you doing here?" Chuck winked. "Looking for a particular lady? Hmm? This might not be the safest place. I hear Lissa's been saying weird things."

August tensed. "About Elle?"

"Nothing about Elle. Just weird shit about you." Chuck scratched his head. "Women. They're hard to figure."

August nodded. A trio of women was walking toward the bandstand, their faces sunburned and laughing, with shopping bags hanging from their arms. They looked at him and Chuck as if they were artwork they'd like to add to their day's purchases. All three had wedding bands on their ring fingers.

August stepped back, but Chuck grinned at them, and they grinned back at him. One of the women slowed, but the others pulled her with them, saying, "Think of Dave."

"I'm on vacation!" she said, and the other two laughed.

Chuck turned to August. "No luck there."

August shook his head. "I think you just had some good luck there because they went away."

"Maybe you're right," Chuck said. "I'm trying to not be dog." He shrugged. "Maybe I better try harder."

August laughed, then an ear-splitting sound came from the microphone on the bandstand behind them.

Chuck groaned. "Is Norman giving another speech? That guy loves the sound of his voice."

August didn't look back. Instead, he was staring ten feet away at Elle, Harper, and Nate, who stood a couple feet away from his co-writer, gesturing toward the bandstand.

August stepped forward to follow them.

"What're you doing?" Chuck asked.

"I'm not sure. I just have this feeling..." August frowned. He couldn't explain it. As if he expected a sudden bad storm. Or a giant shark was going to jump out of the bay and attack people, though sharks didn't swim in the bay waters here.

"What kind of feeling?" Chuck asked.

August shook his head. "Like something bad is going to happen."

Chuck stepped alongside him. "Must be something odd in the air, 'cause I got that same feeling."

He'd barely finished talking when a movement in the corner of August's eye caught his attention. He turned slowly, and his lips flattened. Lissa. Striding straight toward him, cutting in front of the people who were leisurely making their way toward the bandstand. A little girl cried out, and her father yelled, "Hey! You stepped on my daughter's foot."

She didn't slow down. Her face didn't even color with embarrassment. People stepped out of her way to let her through. She wore arrogance like it was her armor.

It was also her downfall, August thought. She'd been raised to believe she was better than other people. She was beautiful and rich, and in her world, that meant she didn't need to be nice or even polite. Those basic qualities weren't necessary parts of her life.

He turned to face her. Ready to get this over with. Done.

She stopped a good foot away from him. "Have you changed your mind?"

He shook his head. He had nothing to say to her.

Raising her voice, she said, "So you meant what you said to me at your chalet?"

"I meant everything I said." He nodded for emphasis.

She took a step back. "Oh, my God, you still

want to kill me," she cried out, her hand over her left breast.

"What the—"

"Stay away from me, August." She held out her hand and pointed her index finger at him. "Stay far away from me, or I'll have to call the sheriff."

He narrowed his eyes and watched her snap around and head toward the bandstand. But before she made the one-eighty turn, he'd seen a tiny smile on her lips.

"She's up to something." August headed toward the bandstand. "I want to see what she's up to."

"That's one crazy bitch," Chuck said, raising his voice to be heard over a crying baby.

Striding fast, August didn't argue.

Fifty-six

On the way to the bandstand, Sylvia heard a baby crying, and over the sound of the crying baby came her son's voice, calling someone a bitch.

Slowing, she glanced behind her. Chuck's best trait was his amiability—a trait neither she nor his father had possessed. She turned forward and forced herself to speed up. She was in disguise and shouldn't look back. Even with a wig and sunglasses and an ugly straw purse one of her guests had left behind after buying a much more attractive tote, she might still be recognized.

But he was her *son*. She had to see what he was talking about.

Before she could turn again, Lissa stomped past her, toward the bandstand. Sylvia strode after her. Mystery solved. Now she knew the cause of the bitch warning.

A lot of people seemed to be heading toward the bandstand but most weren't in a hurry. It was early, and the band wasn't even setting up their instruments yet. No one really wanted to hear Norman talk about how wonderful it was to live in Trouble Bay as either a year-round resident or just a few months out of the year. All the while, not mentioning that he owned a large amount of properties, condos, and apartments in the area.

It used to be funny. Knowing what she now knew, she wasn't laughing anymore. Instead, she focused on keeping Lissa in her view as the younger woman marched onward, people jumping out of her way, except for one small boy who didn't see her.

She rammed right into him.

The boy cried out, falling. The mother screamed and caught him, but Lissa kept going. She never looked back.

Another crime to chalk up to John Norman and his snooty wife. A bad-parenting crime.

Sylvia slowed as the mother picked up the boy and hugged the child against her chest. Two women and a middle-aged man gathered around the mother and child.

Sylvia passed them by. They didn't need her help. Maybe no one did. She'd lost sight of Lissa, but she hurried on toward the bandstand.

Too many people were in her way, and she had to walk around them. She tried to be causal, not wanting to call attention to herself. At least the humidity was down today, so except for her wig-head, the heat was bearable.

When she reached the bandstand, Lissa was stomping up the makeshift wooden steps. Sylvia positioned herself in the middle of the small crowd that had started to gather.

John Norman was standing on the bandstand

already, talking to a group of people who were on the bandstand with him, including his wife, a few board members, and now Lissa.

Sylvia stepped to the second row. With the wig on, no one would recognize her. In front of her was a small girl. She could easily shoot over the child's head and shove the gun back in the straw purse before anyone noticed.

She didn't want to get caught. She certainly didn't want to go to prison. Though this wasn't as well planned as her other two kills, she knew the area and had already mapped out her escape.

She didn't foresee a problem. No one was looking at her now. They were looking at other people who were more interesting: the musicians, the beautiful girls, the beautiful women, younger men, the food shacks, the beautiful sky, even pets...

Dowdy, middle-aged women like she was now were invisible. She could definitely get away with murder in plain sight.

And it wasn't as if she was committing a real crime. She was committing justice.

She'd thought about the journal all night, sleeping restlessly. Her family hadn't been the Normans' only victims. There had been other fires in town besides hers and her ancestors'. Through the years, quite a few other families had suffered from unexpected fires.

She suspected now that arson was the Normans' get-rich and stay-rich remedy, and had been since the first settler who'd also had the first name of Johnathan.

It was unlikely she could prove it. But she *knew*. Knew in every cell of her body that the

Normans were criminals. That they would do anything to get their way.

And she also knew they would never be prosecuted. There was no proof. It was up to her to make sure that vengeance was done. To make the Normans pay for their crimes.

John was striding to the microphone stand now, and she followed him with her eyes. Lissa and Janet pranced behind him, Janet with her simpering smile and Lissa... Well, Lissa still had the crazed look on her face.

Sylvia shivered, then snapped her gaze back to John Norman. He had his avuncular, town board president smile on.

Not for long, she thought, and slid her hand into the ugly purse, finding the gun. Curling her fingers around the warm metal.

The gun felt right within her hand, as if it were in the place it was meant to be. Coming home to mama.

Before she could pull it out of the straw purse, Lissa stepped next to her father. "Daddy! I can't take it anymore." She spoke loudly, half shouting the words. "August threatened to kill me."

John turned to her, his mouth gaping, his complexion blotching with angry red spots. Lissa stepped past him and stopped in front of the microphone on the stand. She faced the crowd of people who were watching her in stunned silence.

"August just wants me to love him." Her voice was plaintive and desperate. She held a tissue below one eye and then the other, as if she were stopping tears. "I can't love him. I *can't*. He said he'll never be arrested. That people won't believe me. Not until after I'm dead."

The murmurs started. Sympathetic murmurs.

"Bullshit," someone called.

Sylvia whipped her head to the source of the voice. Chuck. Standing in the row behind her, toward the left side of the stage. Right next to August, who stood with his arms crossed.

Sylvia pursed her lips. What a fuckup.

She didn't believe Lissa for a nanosecond. But she could see that Lissa had convinced the tourists and perhaps a few townspeople.

"August!" Lissa stood tall, her chin up. Looking brave with her slim body and her model stance. "I'm sick of being afraid. I refuse to hide any longer. And I'm not going to let you kill me."

Then she held out her hand like she had a weapon in it...and sunlight sparkled on the gray metal.

Sylvia gasped. She wasn't the only woman here with a gun. She stared, transfixed like everyone else.

Except two people.

"No!" Elle shouted from somewhere behind Sylvia. "*Noooo!*"

And Chuck shouted, too. "You're fucking crazy!"

It happened fast. Too fast. Chuck stepped in front of August, and out of the corner of her eye, Sylvia saw August raise his arms to push Chuck away.

Too late. Sylvia knew it was too late as she raised her gun and aimed it at Lissa, whose face had lost all the desperation, and there was just the meanness left. The anger. The fury of a woman scorned.

Breathing calmly, concentrating on Lissa, Sylvia pulled the gun all the way out, held her arm out, aimed, then smoothly drew back the trigger.

A bang sounded, and it had an echo, she thought as she winced and jumped. John Norman was yelling, and Sylvia didn't know what he was saying, but Lissa was holding a gun in the air, aimed at Chuck and August.

Lissa slowly toppled, and an odd sound came from her mouth. A kind of pitiful, scared noise. As if she knew she was going to hell.

A terrible scream came from Janet, and an anguished shout came from John. Then Janet was running toward Lissa, falling to her knees. John stumbled after her, and he roared like an injured animal.

Sylvia's breath shuddered, and she looked to the side, but too many people blocked her view of Chuck. She wanted to run to her son, but her legs were weak, and she was shaking.

Why was he here? Why hadn't he stayed away?

She forced herself to take one step, then another and another.

No one pointed to her and said, "There she is! The woman who shot the idiot on the bandstand."

Everyone had probably been looking at Lissa, who'd been giving the message, *Look at me! Look at me!*

No one had been looking at Sylvia.

People surrounded Chuck. She knew she couldn't get to him, but in shock, she still tried to push people out of her way. People turned to stare at her. She could feel them. But all she could think of was Chuck.

Before she could push through, she felt rather than saw someone reaching her side and staying there, and then another person was on her other side.

One of them whisked off the wig; the other grabbed her gun.

She looked left and saw August.

She looked to her right and saw Elle.

"Are we playing a game?" Harper asked, on Elle's other side, holding her mother's hand.

"A fun game," Elle said, and she pulled Sylvia to the right, away from Chuck.

"Chuck," she whispered hoarsely, lagging back.

Everyone was talking excitedly, the air buzzing with voices. But Nate heard her and leaned close, an inch from her ear, his breath on her earlobe. "He'll be okay," he said. "It looks like a flesh wound."

She still lagged back. When she heard "flesh wound" on TV or in a movie, it always turned out to be worse. But something was wrong with her feet and her muscles. They were weak, and she couldn't twist away from August and Elle. Her limbs were so weak that if they hadn't been holding her arms, she thought for sure her legs would collapse.

With another sob, the sound swallowed up by the excited crowd, she allowed Elle and August to lead her away. They walked to her house, almost a mile and a half away, with the adults quiet and Harper talking excitedly. Saying the game they were playing was like games she saw on TV.

They were three blocks away when the wail of a siren came to Sylvia's ears. And then another siren and another siren.

One an ambulance, Sylvia thought. The other two were probably sheriff's cars.

Another siren joined the first two.

Sylvia looked down at Harper, who'd stopped talking, her mouth gaping open.

"Are the police going to arrest you?" Harper asked.

"Of course not," Elle said. "Sylvia didn't do anything wrong. That wasn't a real gun in her hand. That was pretend."

"Like her hair?" Harper asked.

"Yes, like her hair."

Sylvia looked from one to the other. "You knew?"

"Not until after, um..." Elle looked at Harper, then back at Sylvia. "After Chuck was shot."

"I don't think anyone else recognized you," August said.

There were running footsteps behind them. Coming quickly toward them. Coming closer.

She froze. She wanted to run, but her legs were too heavy and too weak. Elle and August stiffened and looked behind them.

"I knew it was you!" Harper laughed, oblivious to the footsteps. This was a game to her. Then her laughter stopped, and she frowned. "I don't want you to go to jail."

"I don't want you do go to jail, either," Nate said, his breaths puffing.

She cried out in relief. He reached out for her and pulled her to him. She hugged him tightly, and he hugged her just as tightly, his chest against hers. She could feel his pounding heartbeat, and she thought he felt hers pounding, too.

Laughing with a sob, she pulled away from him. He had to know what she'd done. So did Elle and August. Yet they were protecting her.

She glanced upward at the sky. It was getting darker now, and the fireworks would go off in another two hours unless someone stopped them.

But she didn't think so. This was a tourist town. They were expecting fireworks, and the town would give them fireworks.

The killing of the town board chairman's daughter would just make it more exciting for them.

"Mommy." Harper tugged the hem of her mother's top. "Can we hide Sylvia?"

Elle laughed shortly. "How about we just tell everyone that Sylvia was with us? Because she is with us. Right?"

Harper nodded. "Yes! She'd right here with us. Now she won't go to jail."

"That's right, honey." Elle stooped and hugged Harper. As she did, she looked at August. "You saw her, too, didn't you?"

He nodded. "The whole time."

Harper pulled away from Elle and put her arms around Sylvia's legs, the top of her head against Sylvia's belly. "I love you," she said. "I won't let the police take you to prison."

"I love you, too." Sylvia's voice was choked as she bent forward to hug Harper. She looked at Elle, who had changed her life more than twenty years ago. Then she looked at Nate, who might not have changed her life but had given her orgasms like she'd never had before. And she looked at August, her son's boss and a man who'd earned her respect. Then she gazed down at the small girl still hugging her tightly. "I love all of you, but I have to find out if Chuck is okay."

"I'll call." August got his phone out and pressed a button. An instant later, he was asking someone how Chuck was doing. He was silent for a moment, then nodded. "So you're saying he'll be all right," he said. "That's good. Real good."

Harper stepped away from Sylvia and clapped her hands. Sylvia went limp, and Nate stepped up, catching her. Leaning her head against his shoulder, she started to sob.

Chuck was going to be all right. Thank God, thank God.

"It's going to be okay," Nate whispered. "It's going to be okay. I haven't known you for long, but you're the bravest woman I know. I think I'm falling in love with you."

She relaxed for a moment against him. She was a strong woman—hadn't she proved how strong she was today? But it felt good to let him hold her up. Just for a little while.

He reminded her of her first rule: Love thyself.

People who loved themselves held themselves up most of the time. But some of the time, they let others hold them up, too.

She only had four rules. Maybe she would make a fifth one. She knew what it would be: *Rule Number Five: Love a man who will lie to the cops for you, make you laugh, and make you feel beautiful and young again.*

"It's all going to be all right," Nate said.

She decided that she liked Rule Number Five a lot.

"As soon as you're ready," he continued, "I'll take you to the hospital."

"I'll have to change first," she said.

He laughed, and her lips turned up, just a little, because nothing had been humorous tonight.

"What about the lady?" Harper asked, her voice high and pitched away from Sylvia, toward Elle. "The mean one. Do you think she's dead?"

"I don't know, sweetie," Elle said. "I don't know."

Against Nate's shoulder, Sylvia's eyes dried. She knew. When she shot at something, she didn't miss. Lissa Norman, the last of the Norman clan, was dead. There would be no more.

The Normans had the money...but she had a son. A living, breathing son.

It didn't make her happy that she'd killed Lissa. Not at all. But she'd been protecting the people she'd loved. And she'd won, damn it. She'd won.

Fifty-seven

August had been in the sheriff's interrogation room for over two hours. They kept saying that they weren't charging him with anything. And he kept saying that he hadn't done anything to be charged with, and he'd certainly never threatened Lissa.

"Then why did she say what she did?"

"I'd broken up with her, and she was used to getting her own way."

The deputy, a heavyset man in his thirties who probably came close to the upper weight limits, scowled. "Then why did she say anything?"

He shrugged and asked for a lawyer. But the Green Bay lawyer he'd asked for was on vacation, and he didn't know any others. Even his vacationing lawyer didn't handle criminal cases. So he decided the hell with it, and he just said he wasn't going to answer any more questions.

Five minutes after ten, the sheriff walked into the room. He sat across from him. "None of this is being recorded."

August just looked at him. He'd watched TV cop shows. No way was he going to believe that.

The sheriff, a tall man with a balding head and a double chin, said, "I got a phone call from an old friend who said you'd broken up with Lissa Norman and were about to marry Elle Styles."

"My dad?"

"Your father knows, too?"

August frowned. This was how they caught criminals. Though his father certainly wasn't a criminal. Neither was Elle, and he leaned over the table, needing to make that clear. "I'm in love with Elle. I want to marry her but haven't asked her yet."

"That's not what her mom told me."

"Mrs. Styles?"

The sheriff smiled wryly. "I was a groomsman at Jenny and Tom's wedding. I don't get to see Elle enough, but I'm her godfather."

August sat straighter. "Elle is special."

"I've lost track of Elle and Jenny. My hours are long, and there's my own family." He shrugged and made a what're-you-gonna-do gesture. "When Jenny called, I had to listen to her. So, you did break up with Lissa?"

"Once Elle came back to town, Lissa and I were done." He shifted in the chair. This was an awkward discussion. "I know that sounds cold, and I'm not proud of it, but Lissa and I..." He shifted again. "Love was never mentioned. It was always just physical."

He looked at the sheriff, who looked back. His lips pressed together. Watching him. Not saying anything. Waiting for something more.

"Everything she said tonight was a lie," August continued. The sheriff wanted more, he would give him more. "She didn't love me. The only thing she'd loved was my father's resort and his money."

There was silence for a few moments, and this time he didn't break it. He'd said what he had to say, and that was it. The clock on the wall clicked loudly. The sheriff balanced the chair on the back two legs, and the chair rocked back and forth, back and forth.

Then he leaned forward, and the front two chair legs smacked down hard on the engineered hardwood floor. He exhaled loudly.

"This is a small community," the sheriff said, "and big fish are noticed in a smaller place. Especially if they're fish who swim around and think they're better than other people. You know what I mean?"

August nodded.

"This isn't for the public record, but we've already gotten a few calls from other people, and they all agree that Lissa had a little crazy in her." He sniffed noisily. "Maybe a lot of crazy. They're saying if I arrest you and you go to court, they'll testify for you. But that's not the reason I'm letting you go."

There was a pause while he got up from the chair slowly. August remained sitting, not saying anything, though he'd been hoping he'd be out of here soon.

"I'm not letting you go because of Jenny or Tom or my goddaughter or all the phone calls saying Lissa Norman was a nutcase." He didn't smile, but the lines around his eyes crinkled. "I'm letting you go because I've got nothing to hold you on."

August stood. He wanted to hug the sheriff, but he restrained himself. "Thank you, Sheriff."

The sheriff nodded, headed to the door, and opened it.

A deputy stood outside, and the sheriff told him to escort him out.

August didn't smile. A woman had died tonight. A woman he'd slept with.

But he wasn't going to mourn her death, either. She'd been ready to do him harm and do harm to the people he knew. She'd shot Chuck. A deputy with a sad face told him that Chuck would be okay, and all August could do was nod and hope he was right.

It was in his past already. He had plans for the rest of his life, and he wasn't going to wait to start putting them into action.

Tonight. His plans were going to start tonight.

Fifty-eight

The mosquitoes were outside, looking for blood, the reason Elle was sitting on August's leather couch in the living room in the dark, her legs curled beneath her as she stared out at the harbor. The official fireworks had stopped an hour ago, but not the unofficial ones. And every once in a while, a firework spiraled or popped or exploded over the lake.

She didn't feel her usual awe and enthusiasm.

Lissa was dead.

And Elle was glad for it. If Sylvia hadn't killed Lissa, and if Chuck hadn't stepped in front of August, Elle had no doubt that Lissa would have killed August and then would have plead insanity.

With a good team of lawyers behind her, she very well could have gotten away with it.

She would have been famous.

She would have loved that.

Elle was sure that Lissa had considered all the possible outcomes and had decided that, yes, they were fine with her.

It made Elle sick.

The doorknob turned. She uncurled her legs, and as the door opened, she stood.

The light turned on. The door closed. August stood in the entranceway, and he stared at her. "Elle."

She smiled. "Welcome home, August."

He didn't smile. For an instant, his face crumbled. Yet, he didn't cry. She was the one who held back tears as he strode to her. Took her in his arms. Held her tightly, as if he never wanted to let her go. Then he loosened his hold and kissed her.

And kissed her.

And kissed her.

When he stopped kissing her, she could see his eyes were dark with emotion, and he still clasped her upper arms.

"I didn't expect you to be here," he said. "I was going to change before going to your place."

"The truth is, I'm tired of waiting for you."

"The truth is," he replied, "I'm tired of waiting for me, too."

"It stops tonight." She jutted her chin at him. "I'm taking control."

He smiled slowly. "You are, huh? And what are you going to do about it?"

"I think... I'm going to find a job in the area. Or make my own job. I have a few ideas."

He nodded.

"And housing," she added. "I'm going to find housing."

"That's the easy part. I have room. If you want something bigger, we can look for something bigger. Big enough for all of us." He kissed her forehead, and his voice lowered. "And maybe a puppy for Harper."

Tears started, and she blinked them away. She was *not* going to cry. "I don't care if the house is big or not."

"What about the ring? You want a big one, right? Women do. At least, so I've heard."

"A ring?" Her voice wobbled, and she swallowed.

"An engagement ring." He bent down to kiss her softly on the lips. As if she were something precious.

Nice, she thought. But she preferred the earlier passionate kiss.

She put her hand on the side of his face. "It's not the size that I care about." She smiled and glanced downward, below his waistline, then up again. "Though your size is certainly...admirable."

He grinned, then he laughed, pure joy in his voice and on his face.

She grinned back at him, feeling happiness beam out from her. As his laughter slowed, the corners of her lips pulled down, and she pushed out of his loose grip, stepping back from him.

"It's the love that I care about," she said. "Your love. I don't want you to do this out of relief or a sense of payback. I want you to do this out of crazy love. And if you don't feel that way about me, the best way you can repay me is to be honest and then say good-bye."

"Elle, I—"

"I'm not done." She held her head high. "There won't be any recriminations or anger. It will be okay. But I want the real thing. Real man-woman love, not gratitude and I-don't-mind-fucking-you love."

"You want the truth, hmmm?"

She nodded. Whatever he said, she could take it. "The truth."

"The truth is"—his lips curved up—"I've loved you since the day I first met you. You were my shining star. My bright sun. You were pure light, and you won my heart. You've had it all these years, and I've never wanted it back."

"I *helped* you and your mom. You were only eight. What you felt was gratitude, not love."

"You're wrong." He shook his head, his gaze on her unfaltering. "It was more than gratitude. You were my angel. And then years later, the first time I saw you as an adult, I helped you give birth."

Tears prickled her eyes. He was doing it again. Making her want to cry. "That's always a romantic moment. Asking me to marry you right after a baby was pushed out of my vagina."

He laughed, and she could see the happiness in his face. "If I hadn't been deployed soon after, I would have wooed you."

"You shouldn't have waited so long."

His expression sobered. "You were busy with your classes. You would've said no again."

She frowned. He was right, but for the wrong reasons. "I wouldn't have believed that you loved me. I would have put it down as gratitude."

"I didn't fight for you. I held back. You deserve a fighter, and I'm fighting now."

"I understand that you were deployed," she said, "but you weren't deployed forever. After you came home this last time, you didn't come for me. I know it was rough for you, but it's better if you talk about it."

He didn't answer her right away, frowning. Then he exhaled a long breath. "I think I'd like that. From now on, we'll talk."

She put her arms around him.

He slid his arms around her and held her tightly. From the lake came the distant boom of a firework. "You make fireworks go off inside me," he whispered.

She laughed. "That's the sweetest thing you've said to me."

"The corniest," he said. "And it's true. You make me smile. When I'm with you, my heart is happy."

She kissed him on his chin, then next to his mouth. "That's good. Go on. Keep it up."

"You asked for it, and here it is." His voice lowered and warmed. "When I'm not with you, I think of you as my guiding light. It's only after this last deployment that it was hard for me to conjure up that light again. But now it's back. And now you're back. I don't want to miss you again."

She sighed and laid her head on his shoulder. This was good. She didn't think it would get much better.

"I want to be a husband to you," he continued, "and a father to Harper. And if it's okay with you, I wouldn't mind having more children with you."

She sighed happily. Okay, it just did get better. She lifted her head. "Harper will be a great big sister. But not right away, please."

He tilted his head down to kiss her.

She pulled away first, leaving one hand on his shoulder. "I've loved you since we first met, too."

He looked at her, waiting. His eyes patient and filled with love. So much, it hurt her chest. A joyful hurt.

"We were separated," she said.

"Like a boy and girl in a fairy tale," he said.

"A fairy tale?" She smiled.

He grinned back at her. "Duke used to read fairy tales to me. His mother had read them to him, and he'd saved the books for his children." He paused. "He also read books for boys. I'll read the fairy tales to Harper. And when you and I have our children, I'll read to them, too. I know that Harper has a father—"

"Who rarely sees her," Elle said.

His mouth straightened, and he looked into her eyes. "I was there at her birth. I love her like she's my own."

She sniffed back tears. Her heart ached with them. Ached with happiness. A woman had died today, and Elle thought that perhaps she shouldn't say that it was the happiest day in her life...but it was.

If she had died instead of Lissa, Lissa would be calling her friends to throw a party.

But she didn't want to think about her anymore. Lissa had never been her obstacle or her problem. She and August had created their own obstacles. Their own problems.

They'd taken the obstacles away... And now the gates of love were wide open, and they were crossing through.

She laughed with pure happiness. "I love you," she said. "I love *you*."

"Tell me you'll marry me. Tell me you'll love me when I'm old and grouchy."

"I will. And when we're old, I'll still make you smile."

He kissed her then, and it was like the fireworks. Bright and fiery and hot. Unlike the fireworks outside, it would be that way year round.

And tonight. Tonight she was going to be one very lucky woman.

"Let's make love," she said.

"You always did have the best ideas." As he held her close, he whispered, "Life is good."

Not just good, she thought. Life was great. And love...she sighed happily...love was wonderful.

Thank you so much for reading *Rules of Love & Murder, book 2* in my Love & Murder series. The next book, *A Love & Murder Christmas*, will be available in October. It has a sick girl, a pooka in the form of a five-foot-two talking cat, the girl's worried single father, and a sympathetic woman—who happens to be the widow of Paul Finney (the crooked insurance agent who met an untimely death in *Rules of Love & Murder*).

It also has a would-be murderer.

To stay updated on new releases, special sales and giveaways, sign up for my newsletter. www.edieramer.com/newsletter.

About the Author

A *USA Today* bestselling author, Edie is funnier on the page than in real life. She writes stories with heart, attitude, and suspense. She lives in Wisconsin with her husband and one very important cat. She's happy to be able to do what she loves nearly every day.

Edie loves hearing from readers. You can visit her at www.edieramer.com and easily email her at http://edieramer.com/contact.

Acknowledgments

I'm blessed to have Amy Atwell and the Author E.M.S. team helping me through this publishing process. They make it almost easy. Lately, I've needed them more than ever. Amy is an amazing, shining star, and I'm lucky to know her.